Born and raised on a farm in Lincolnshire, the author led a restless youth, emigrating to Australia where she earned a degree in arts and social science from the University of Sydney. She went on to work in the prison system as a parole officer before focusing on writing. Over the years, her articles and short stories have been published in various magazines, many during the rise of women's liberation in the 1970s. She published a collection of short stories, *Passing the Baton,* in 2012, followed by her debut novel, *Curtains,* in 2016.

Now living in Herne Bay, she thanks the local writing group at Beach Creative as a stimulating creative influence.

# Dedication

After many years working as a parole officer in NSW, Australia, I'm grateful to my former colleagues and, in several cases, certain prisoners.

Jean Ramm

# SEARCHING, FINDING, LOSING

AUSTIN MACAULEY PUBLISHERS™

LONDON • CAMBRIDGE • NEW YORK • SHARJAH

A CIP catalogue record for this title is available from the British Library.

ISBN 9781035842926 (Paperback)
ISBN 9781035842933 (ePub e-book)

www.austinmacauley.com

First Published 2024
Austin Macauley Publishers Ltd®
1 Canada Square
Canary Wharf
London
E14 5AA

# Acknowledgments

Many thanks to Beach Creative, Herne Bay, Kent, for their stimulating writing groups.

# Table of Contents

# Part 1

Jane was at the funeral – Martin's, to be precise – he was, in a sense, her ex. Dead now. Finished.

His mother approached and introduced, 'And this is Maria…' she said, gesturing to a young woman beside her.

Jane replied, 'Pleased to meet you,' looking straight into the eyes of this female, the one who had taken him from her, who was now nodding and smiling at her. Jane didn't give her a chance to respond and looked at his now tearful mother. Then the coffin moved along slowly and everyone went quiet standing still, eyes focussed on the hearse. Afterwards, Jane decided to go briefly to his parents' house for a memorial gathering –that's what his mother referred to it as. She was partly intrigued by the process, having never been to a funeral before and at the same time aware that she didn't have a real place in all this. Well, not really.

It was a grand detached house in the Chelsea area – large garden at the rear, two garages and five or six bedrooms along with an expansive conservatory. Over the years she'd visited with Martin but only occasionally. He never seemed to want to hang around there and she'd backed him on that. He'd joked about being an only child. Of course, she was also – though in a slightly different way.

Jane took a glass of claret and looked across at Maria, who was diligently attending to Martin's mother. She approached Jane again, saying, 'Jane, I hardly saw him for years, my son, but I was always hoping for a grandchild…and she's good.' Her gaze was fixed on Maria. *So, she's surpassing me, is she?* Jane thought, as his mother went on, 'I need help…still suffering from shock about Martin but hopefully a baby…'

Tears were welling up again. Jane noticed Maria was starting to serve sherry now to all the elderly relatives. 'You, Jane, you were with him for years…up there in the north.' More dabbing of eyes before his mother moved away and Jane gulped down her glass of wine seeing Maria was now handing round mince pies. *What a pregnant bitch,* Jane thought, looking at that slightly rising stomach. She finished the claret, her mouth tightening.

She moved for a mince pie and picked up a glass of sherry from the table, then looking across again at Maria. She was a very small woman whose face was round, her mouth so tiny, her legs looking swollen right down to the ankles area.

Then Mark's father clinked a gong-like thing and the room went quiet.

'I'm afraid I have something very serious to announce.'

Jane was near the door and thought, *It's time for me to go.* She left quietly, seeing her Jaguar car across the road. The sight pleased her. She crossed and flopped in smiling to herself as she moved away with her foot on the accelerator. At times, actions spoke louder than words. Where had she come across that saying before? She hooted at a mother with three young children crossing the road next to the school. No doubt it was going to be a pedestrian crossing, so the local paper would say, but it wasn't yet.

She drove out of town, eventually halting to purchase fish and chips. Seated within her cherished vehicle, she indulged in the meal. They'd first met, years ago, in that well-known pub on a Friday night when she was alone having a G and T, thinking that some of her work colleagues might turn up. She felt someone touched her bottom as he went to the bar and then he came back with his drink and apologised. He was much older than her and his suit looked perfectly tailored. They started to talk and he suggested they should go out for a meal. More wine. She had had the occasional 'one off' and that was how she thought of it, and that's what happened with him that night, but it didn't end there and, somehow, they became, what some would say as, partners.

In those early days, she had different office jobs. Her birthplace was a vast council estate area in East London, where she was raised on the 19th floor. She left her comprehensive school just before she was 16, feeling determined to get a future for herself – move away from council estates. Initially, she relocated to a local bedsit, sharing bathroom, kitchen and toilet with other tenants. Then her salary increased and she moved to a flat in what she thought of as slightly better than her birth area. The expenses of which took most of her earnings, so it wasn't long before she got a tenant to share with her.

*Stop it! Stop it! I'm going over all this unnecessarily. I know it. I know it. I've clambered up that ladder and I'm still on the way up. Going higher. Higher.*

*Martin. Martin. My mistaken saviour. My traitor. I can still see that Maria bitch graciously serving the mourners, assisting his mother, Gladys, who gloated to me about Maria's pregnancy, with that "and look what you never did" expression. Thank fucking Christ I never did…and never will. Who wants children when they've got my life?*

She looked at her watch. 'Time to move on.' She sighed. Had Martin, at times, seemed like the father she had never known, being so much older than her? Yes, their initial physical involvement had seemed more pragmatic than pleasurable for her, while for him, it appeared essential. It was all the dosh he had and she felt herself moving into it all. Clearing out of Tower Hamlets, moving to a completely different place. His good job. Secure money. 'Come on, come on,' she told herself. 'Get back. Get back to Lincoln. Fingers crossed. Fingers crossed. Get on with the present.' Yet her thoughts started their journey back.

Her single mother, as she was always seen, passed away a year after she'd left school. Breast cancer. Jane took a portion of fish. The batter was delicious. Hmm…she hadn't been the best mother in the world. More likely the worst. All those blokes who started coming to their flat, she recalled, and the one who came into her bedroom late that evening. Stop it. Stop it. You were only a child. Now you're a woman and there's more good things on the card. Well, hopefully. You escaped. Did well.

Now was the moment to head back up north, to the place she now called hers. Well not "their place" but "her place", was it? Anyway, it wasn't really north, it was midlands. His mother always called it north, as so many Londoners did. This

14

place is Lincoln, which, yes, was hopefully her place now. She smiled, fastening her seat belt and that lovely villa in the south of France. Same. She pulled out of the carpark using her debit card to exit, tossing her fish and chip wrapping paper out of the window.

It was all in her mind as she drove on. Life was strange. Sometimes things emerged unexpectedly. Like Rob. She'd known him for nearly a year before it all started. Wow! Seems life is like that, often seeming like flowers in springtime and then comes autumn and the beautiful petals start to wrinkle and then fall. Indeed, it was autumn now, even moving fast heading out of London and she could see some of the trees were beginning to look on the bare side. Of course, there were others that didn't crumble. They stood up to changes in temperature and decline of sunshine.

*********************

Feeling tired an hour later, she stopped on the A1 for coffee, sitting down in a service station café, surrounded by chatting people. Her thoughts were on Rob as she sipped her cappuccino. Then a guy came up to her, saying, 'Can I share your table?' Taking a quick look around she noted the tables were all occupied. She nodded, her thoughts on Rob continuing as she stirred her coffee. There was something about him and their relationship but she wasn't sure what it was.

'Always the same here,' this chap said giving her that full on look. 'Where you heading?'

'Lincs,' she said, telling herself to stop looking at his lovely thighs as he sat with one each side of the table leg. Like

Rob's. Like Rob's. He looked at his watch and suddenly gulped down his expresso.

'Shit. Have to go. Running late.' He stood up and looked at her with a friendly grin, his eyes widening.

'You want a lift anywhere?' She grinned back and shook her head then watched through the window as he crossed by the petrol tanks to get into his car…a boring middle-sized KIA. It gave her a flood of confidence as she moved her eyes to her parked Jaguar.

\*\*\*\*\*\*\*\*\*\*\*\*\*\*\*\*\*\*\*\*\*

# Part 2

Jane had continued to meet Martin after that 'one off'. He'd said again and again that he really enjoyed it but Jane's sex life wasn't that simple. She could never stop thinking about the physical, the biological side of it all while it was in progress and never felt any intense pleasure. However, he provided her with other pleasures. He seemed wealthy and well-established and she became encapsulated with a sense of the privileges he seemed to be offering.

Martin had clearly wanted their relationship to persist and started saying he'd love to take her to what he called "my pad", which was way out of London. His time in London was always brief and to do with his work. When they met, it was always in whatever hotel he was booked in, frequently starting with a meal in, what she regarded as an expensive restaurant. He did suggest once that she take him to her flat but the problem there was that she now shared it with another girl who was always around. Eventually she agreed to travel to his place, what she thought of as the north, but as he said, it was Midlands.

On the big day, he drove her out of London in what she saw as a "posh" car. They arrived at his lovely large apartment in the ancient area of Lincoln and from the window you could see the Cathedral standing magnificently and hear the bells being tolled. He gave her that friendly look and said, 'Good to get away?'

She wasn't sure what he meant and said, 'Err. I've got to go back, of course.'

'Of course,' he replied giving her that friendly grin as he moved to make them a coffee.

Watching him grind the beans she started to wonder how old he was. There were times when, for some reason, she thought about the father she never had. Never knew. Could have been anybody. Other times he gave her lots of teacher-like information. Now, he was talking about the periods of development in Lincoln, the Romans, the Normans but she wasn't listening properly. She hadn't been out and about but already she was feeling intrigued by what he said was a small city.

They did, as she expected, have sex that night in his large double bed and then again on the next day, Sunday, before he drove her back to East London where her flat and her office job was.

'Look, think about it,' he said. 'You could move up to Lincoln and get a job. Share my apartment.'

He kissed her as she got out of the car and she knew she was one hundred percent attracted to his suggestion. He drove off wondering if she'd ever been out of London before her trip to Lincoln. He was right to wonder. Her only time out of London was once on a school trip to Southend-on-Sea.

\*\*\*\*\*\*\*\*\*\*\*\*\*\*\*\*\*\*\*\*

The next week he rang her frequently and she began to have a surge of enthusiasm about moving to a new place, not to mention being with a man like him – privileged, good job, talked about having played golf, parents in Chelsea. He was older than her but it seemed inappropriate to ask him his age, But she intended to, yes, she intended to ask. Another thing was that he was not very tall and a little on the plump side.

Martin began to feel he might have found a potential partner. She listened to him and seemed to like his apartment. He'd had a restless time growing up, being an only child, his parents being more than a little on the clinging side, especially his mother. In the earlier years, he had been involved with Sarah, but their relationship fizzled out as she grew too close to his mother, and that contradicted his desire for independence. This occurred during a period when his father, who was a solicitor, always wanted his son to go into law, which he'd started out doing, but soon felt it wasn't for him. He'd moved to more business type work which had taken time but had lasted for years and was now soaring ahead. He had owned the Lincoln place for three years.

'Hi, Martin.' It was Jane on his mobile.

'Oh, Jane, hello.'

'I've applied for a job in Lincoln.'

'You have? That's great.'

'Martin, are you at work now?'

'Well, yes, but not in the office. Just packing the car ready.'

'Where you…'

'Horncastle.'

She'd never heard of that place.

19

'Business stuff. But please come as soon as you can. There's a good train service.'

'Well, I'll wait to see if I get an interview.'

'Okay, I'll be back home tomorrow – staying over in Horncastle for afternoon and evening meetings.'

'Thanks, Martin.'

She put the phone down and left her desk, heading for the little office kitchen to make a cup of tea. This was a big step. Stop it. Don't start doubting. Her mobile rang.

'Jane. I'd love you to come. Where's the job you've applied for?'

'Can't talk, Martin. At work. More later.'

Martin got in his car taking Jane's news with him. She was young, not necessarily innocent but she'd grown up in that tough area of London. Her accent remained a factor, and its reception during a potential interview in Lincoln was uncertain, depending on the specific location. It could be a bonus in certain jobs. Perhaps one day she'd invite him to meet her parents – well, probably not, and he wasn't too eager to rush her to meet his. He could give her a lot and she, well, she had a body to die for. All those years he'd had no sex, now it was well and truly on again. Seemed work, on its own, no matter how profitable it was becoming, was not enough. Now he could see he had advantages coming along, something he was definitely going to build on.

\*\*\*\*\*\*\*\*\*\*\*\*\*\*\*\*\*\*\*\*

They were in a restaurant near his apartment. Orders made, wine first sips.

'Mustn't drink too much, Martin. I have an interview tomorrow at 9.30.' Jane looked across at him with those lovely brown eyes and the dark eye lashes.

'That's okay, any unfinished wine we can take home. I do it sometimes when I'm on my own.'

'I've got another job interview for next week.'

'Ah, great. Can you stay over, as they say these days?'

'Yes, I think…'

'I'll be away for two nights next week but I'd love you to stay.'

'Not sure but I'll check and let you know.' He raised his glass.

'Cheers…'

He looked at her seriously as they clinked glasses.

'I've had some good news. My uncle, Dad's brother, has died and left me something in his will.'

'Lucky you.'

'Yeah…'

A hush fell over them as they commenced their first course. Jane was looking around in a casual way at the other people occupying tables, her thoughts on what she would feel if she was lucky like him. She didn't have any uncles. Is that what uncles did?

'Did you know he was going to leave you money?'

'Err…no idea. Mind you, he was a real loner. No wife.'

'I see.'

'You have any uncles?'

Well, she wasn't in the mood to talk about her family. Family? Was it family?

She didn't have one.

'Delicious food, Martin.'

'Yeah, good place this is. A drop more? Come on, it's only,' he looked down at his watch, 'nine o'clock.'

'You've already poured it.' She grinned, her eyes meeting his. She knew what his plan was for later.

He sipped more wine, preparing to make dessert choices as he reached for the menu.

'Big decisions here, Jane.'

'I'm easy, Martin. You decide.'

While he concentrated on making a decision, a process that always seemed challenging for him, his attention shifted to Jane and could feel some stirring in his body. Awakening. She was going to be his tonight. That was for sure. He tried not to think about her body, telling himself to peruse the dessert menu. There were at least 3 which he would like.

After their cream trifle desserts, Jane started to think she would stay until her second interview next week, as she was due to have some time off from her present job in London. She teased herself thinking Martin wasn't the most handsome man in the world and he was greying a bit. Was his height a disadvantage? Well, perhaps he was a touch taller than her except it was when she wore her medium-high heels that she felt they were on a level. Perhaps she should be wary and not do what she did tonight; wear these stiletto heels. How old was he? Didn't want to know that. Not now anyway. He was paying the bill and including a generous tip for the waitress.

It was sex, as they both expected, that night. What she regarded as his sex and she remained nestled to him until 7.00am when she awoke and got up making tea for them both.

\*\*\*\*\*\*\*\*\*\*\*\*\*\*\*\*\*\*\*\*

22

Her interview at the estate agents went well and leaving her with a sense of confidence about relocating from her London neighbourhood to live here, regardless of whether she secured the job or not. Leaving that place embedded with high rise living areas and the miserable sound and smell of roaring, oozing traffic. Idea of moving enthralled her. This was only a small city but it was charming her – that enormous cathedral, the old castle remains and Martin's apartment was close to all these ancient things. Then down the steep hill there was an abundance of shops, art galleries, cinemas and hairdressers. She was certainly going to ponder to all his needs. She'd never really enjoyed sex but it was clear to her that men wanted it and it was, therefore, always a bonus. All she wanted was for him to feel the delights of what she thought of as "sperming into her". Thank goodness she'd had that thing fitted ages ago so there was no chance of pregnancy.

After his two nights away, Martin returned home seeming delighted to greet her.

'Do you know, Jane, I missed you so much in Horncastle. Couldn't stop thinking about you being alone here in my bed.'

'Well, I'm finding the place great and so different from what I'm used to.'

'I can take a day off today. Let's go for a drive somewhere.'

'I'd like that.'

'The Wolds.'

'The what?'

They laughed and he explained where it was. 'I've got a cottage there. Had it for quite a while now. Got it before I got this place and lived there for a few months. Now I rent it out.'

'What is it?'

'Cottage. Lovely spot.'

She looked down at her scrambled egg, trying not to seem excited.

Later that day as they drove east out of Lincoln in his splendid Rolls Royce, she had a recorded message on her mobile.

'You've got the job. When can you start? In two weeks' time we hope. We've written a letter to your address confirming everything. Please, reply asap.'

She looked across at Martin. Unlike her, he'd never used his mobile when they were on the move.

'I've got the job.'

'Well done…'

'Start in two weeks.'

He pulled over into a country lane and put his arm across, gently stroking her neck, grinning,

'Join me then…I'll welcome you.'

'Hmm.' She pondered over it all as they drove on into a very rural area and she became absorbed by hills and tiny snuggling villages.

'It goes on for miles,' he said.

She tried to cope with a feeling of excitement, noting all the village names. Scramblesby, Bag Enderby, Belchford, Burgh on Bain, Welton le Wold.

By the time they eventually stopped for lunch in an old pub, The Royal Oak, she felt very dreamlike. He ordered a steak but unusually she went for a cheese salad. Her stomach was a bit uncomfortable.

'I can't eat it all. Please, share some.'

He did, and they continued on their drive, had quick look at his little cottage, nestling in the hillside. Couldn't go in as

24

it was rented out for 2 weeks. Back in Lincoln early evening. She went to bed before him and was asleep when he joined her.

She awoke before him and touched his penis, something which suddenly made her feel in control. He awoke and his erection was soon happening. She relaxed. He penetrated. All seemed the same.

'Of course, I've got to head back today.'

'Yes, I know.'

She got up and made a mug of tea for them both.

'Jane, I've been thinking. I'll come to London when you're ready to move places. As you know, I've a lot of spare space here. You can bring all your belongings.'

After that, she couldn't stop looking around the place, the various rooms, thinking of the things she would bring.

\*\*\*\*\*\*\*\*\*\*\*\*\*\*\*\*\*\*\*\*\*

Back in London she told the other occupant who shared the flat with her.

'I'm moving out of here with this new bloke.'

'Any photo of him?' Sue asked. Jane shared one she had on her mobile.

'Heck. How old is he?'

'I don't know.'

'Not a good photo…makes him look more like a father.'

She didn't answer and they talked about a new occupant who worked in the office that Jane would be leaving. 'She's keen to move in and take my place here.'

'Well, keep in touch.'

'Yeah, I will.'

The next week Martin turned up at the flat, helping her to pack everything and then carry it out to his car in the underground carpark. He'd come in his Range Rover which she hadn't seen before. He was feeling full of energy and enthusiasm as if he was achieving an award, but then telling himself to be more cautious.

She looked out of his car as they moved away from this densely populated, high rise area with the loud noise of traffic and crowded pavements, then supermarkets, train stations, queues of people often waiting for red lights to give them safety crossing the road. Then she wound up her window and closed her eyes. Thoughts of her mother flashed into her mind and her mouth tightened.

'Jane. You go into your bedroom and do your homework.'

'I've done it.'

'Then get outside and…'

'I want to watch telly.'

'Well, you can't. I've got visitors coming.'

So, she'd got customers again or that's what she liked to call them sometimes. Times like this she could always smell alcohol on her breath.

'You all right, Jane? You're looking a bit err…sad or miserable.'

'Yeah. Am okay. Just thinking.'

'Worrying about if you've got everything?'

'No. Just thinking about my mother. We just passed that high rise where I lived. Well, not just, we're well away now.'

'Yeah, you've mentioned her…and you had no father.'

She hadn't really told him about her mother. Just that she had one, thinking, Mother. You bitch. You, body seller.

'Correct.' She looked round at him and her spirits began to rise. He was concentrating on the driving, the direction, for him, a different way out of London. He thought about the town they were heading for and all the ruralness of the county where he now worked. His dad had said, 'It's all ploughed fields and green pastures,' not a bad point but not a particularly good one. His dad's tone had made it all sound dull and dreary which wasn't right. Yes, and bear in mind, London had a lot of positives but negatives too.

He took a quick look at Jane, then thought of his long-time ex. Sarah. Three pregnancies she had after they split up and the father of her children turned out to be a former colleague of his from work – a man named Charlie, whom she had met at a work Christmas event. God only knows what some people want.

Now he had those extra thousands from Uncle Edgar and he'd been looking into that villa in the South of France. He'd take Jane there to view the place and see what she thought. He glanced across at her and saw she was sitting with her eyes closed, probably having a nap after all the packing. He decided to let her rest.

Jane, however, was back in Tower Hamlets thinking of her single mother, as she was known by some. She'd died a year after her daughter left school at 16. Breast cancer they said. Hmmm. Not the best mother in the world, more like the worst. All those blokes, her mother's customers, who started coming to their flat, all this she still recalled and the one who came into her bedroom late that evening when she'd shut herself away, prepared for bed, where she was going to sit up and do some of her homework. Then he'd entered her room and turned the key, locking the door. Looking back afterwards she wished she'd locked it. Lesson learnt. Then he'd unzipped his fly and forced her thighs to open, sticking his penis in, then leaving her a £20 and a £5 note and five one-pound coins on the bedside cabinet. Sometime later, looking back, she recalled thinking her virginity was well and truly over and that he'd done something he shouldn't have done but looking back, at the time, there had been some pleasure in having the £30. Told no one. It was likely her mother knew.

All that happened when she was just eleven. Years later she'd had sex with different men, usually one-offs as she always thought of them. She'd often joked there'd be a cost and was occasionally given money. Never saw herself as looking for a long-term relationship, but, but…

********************

On arrival at his place, Martin helped with all the luggage placing it into a small spare upstairs room which, initially, was virtually empty. No bed in there but there was a desk. Now it was full of her possessions, a lot was just clutter which now she'd get rid of in charity shops or rubbish dumps.

'Any photos of your mum?' he said, as he looked at a picture of Jane in her school uniform.

'Certainly not.'

He left her to it and sat at the dining room table taking his business work out of his briefcase and opening his laptop.

Jane began to feel exhausted but made herself labour on, finding another photo of herself on a school trip to Southend and hanging it on the wall. 15 then, 7 years ago. Her mother

28

had died soon after she'd moved to a flat and she had no idea what happened to her dead body. She'd told the hospital she wasn't interested. Come on, Jane, she told herself. You know she was a prostitute. Not like you, you've got skills and can get paid, if a little, for office work. Leaving the room, she approached Martin.

'Can I have a G and T?'

'Yep. I'll get you one.'

'Bring it to me then.' She went back into the room trying to focus herself on clothes, cosmetics and her old cassette player and then putting on a Simon and Garfunkel.

Martin entered with her drink and responded to the music by doing a little dance, moving his hips and trying to swing his shoulders, then winking at her as he turned at the door to leave the room. She tried to amuse herself when he'd gone sipping her drink and thinking, *I grew up in a brothel.*

That night they had sausage and mash, which they made together and, by the time they ate, along with drinking cider, Jane laughed as Martin kept getting up and doing bits of dance movement.

'Oh, by the way, on Sunday I'm taking you to my parents place for a Sunday lunch.'

'Martin.' She looked across the table. 'Can we leave that until I'm settled into work and all that…in'it better to do that…' He chewed his sausage and started to nod.

'You could take me to look inside your cottage in the… er…'

'The Wolds. Yes, no problem. Let's do that.'

He seemed relieved and joked saying, 'In'it better sometimes to change plans.' She didn't seem to notice he was playing with her accent.

*********************

It would soon be 2 years since she arrived in Lincoln. Martin continued his business work, some of which was connected to farmers, like tractors, trailers, ploughs, etc. etc., and his new partner, as he called her, continued to be a bonus. She'd settled into her work here at the Estate Agents and so far had never returned to London.

'Jane,' he said as they were having Sunday lunch in the local Inn, 'we're going to France. You must have some leave; you've been working there for over a year now.'

'Yes, I have. Sounds good.'

She knew it was to do with the money he'd inherited some time ago now and he had talked a lot about purchasing a place there.

A month later they flew there and she was captivated with the riviera coast, the sunshine, beautiful beaches, blue sea, al fresco dining.

'I feel I'm having a dream,' she said, as they peered out over their hotel room balcony.

'Me too,' he said and he winked at her. She knew he was referring to the new bikini she'd been wearing, which, to her surprise, had a very comfortable, low waist, thong. She'd brought her old bikini as well in case the thong was too tight but it turned out to be comfortable.

They decided to go for the first villa they saw, a place Martin had been looking into online for some time with a local Estate Agent in the UK.

'It's perfect,' Jane said, 'and I love Antibes.'

'Well, it's for us, Jane. Something we can share. From my uncle.'

'Will it be in my name too?'

'Of course,' he said, 'let's get to the beach.'

*And get my bikini on,* she thought, knowing that after a swim and short lie in the sun, they'd be back in the hotel for sex.

So, the villa was purchased and over the next year they went four times, once for a whole week, and other times for long weekends.

*********************

By the time they decided to visit his parents, they'd been together for nearly three years. It was planned for what Martin described as their usual Sunday lunch and Jane tried to make sure she wore the right clothes like the jacket and the high-necked white blouse which she wore for work.

'It'll be warm in their place, so you'll have to take your jacket off.'

'I'm ready for that.'

'Think you'll enjoy the meal'

'Yes. Sunday lunches were not a particular thing when I grew up,' she said, thinking Sunday was a busy time for that woman whose customers rolled in on that day.

'Hmm...you'll enjoy it. We've had it here but nearly always in evenings.'

'Ah, you're right but we've had it in pubs once or twice or more, haven't we?'

She got up to clear their breakfast table and he rose and started doing his dance to some music on the radio before assisting her in the kitchen.

Jane enjoyed the drive into that area of London, where she'd hardly ever been before. All the elegant lines of ancient houses all spruced up and giving out the message, 'We're privileged, we deserve it, we live here.'

His mother met them as they walked into the hall.

'Hang your clothes through there.'

'Mum. This is Jane.'

'Pleased to meet you, Jane.' She held out her hand and Jane responded, feeling afterwards that she was too tense and probably gripped it too hard. They moved into the lounge where Martin's father got up from his armchair and greeted them, fixing his attention on his son.

'Obviously enjoying Lincoln, are you?'

'Yep. We are, Dad.'

'You know I'm retired now, boy.'

'Playing golf a lot?' Martin winked at Jane.

'Lucky you, I don't do that much these days. Perhaps when I retire.'

Jane shuffled uneasily wondering if she should go to the kitchen and see if his mother needed help but his dad said assertively,

'Sit down, both of you.'

He went over to the fireplace and put another log on. Jane and Martin sat together on the settee and she couldn't take her eyes off the fire flaring up around the logs with smoke pouring up to the chimney. Never seen such a thing before except in films. Then her eyes turned to all the ancient looking vases, around the place. They'd cost a fortune if they were sold. Martin had told her that his father had been a solicitor. He'd worked with many lawyers and seemed to know everything there was to know about law.

'You like living up there?' Charles said looking at her.

'Yes, I love it.'

His mother was behind the settee now, saying, 'Yes, Charles – she came from Tower Hamlets.'

'Tower Hamlets!'

'Yes, I told you, dear. Anyway, lunch is ready, come through.'

Jane enjoyed the lamb but wasn't sure about the mint sauce, although she ate it. As a child she'd refused to eat it in the school canteen and got some surprising looks from that teacher who always sat with them. Martin chatted to his parents about his work, the agricultural side of it and the usefulness of choosing the most likely products to be sold in that place, where farms were in abundance.

'Lovely roast potatoes,' Jane said and his mother looked up and nodded.

'Probably from Lincolnshire,' Martin said.

'Really. Lincolnshire!' His mother gave him a curious look.

There was silence while all concentrated on their eating, then his mother looked across at Jane.

'Jane, you're young. What are your plans?'

'Plans! Don't think I have any.'

'Ever think about having a family?'

Jane struggled to swallow her last piece of lamb.

Martin interrupted saying, 'You know we've got that lovely villa in the south of France. What I got after Uncle Edgar left me thousands in his Will.'

Another pause. Uncle Edgar, Dad's bother had never been a favourite with his parents but had always been friendly with him when he was a boy, several times taking him to pantomimes. and once to a circus. Then he seemed to vanish.

No one said anything but after he'd downed his roast Charles commented on Edgar and how he had managed not to fight in the Second World War.

Gladys looked around at them all.

'Should they come back to London?' She spoke looking at her husband but he didn't respond.

'Did you hear me, Charles?'

'What dear? Yes, I heard.'

He picked up his glass and finished his Guiness.

'I'll get you another, Dad.' Martin stood up.

'He doesn't want it,' Gladys said. 'You only like one, don't you dear?'

Charles laughed. 'These days, yes.'

Martin poured more wine into Jane's glass and then his own. Yes, his dad enjoyed his Guiness and his mother hardly ever drank alcohol, perhaps the occasional sherry if she was with others of her age.

The pudding came next and they all enjoyed the apple and blackberry pie with dollops of whipped cream.

'We don't drink coffee at this time but I know Martin does.'

'Don't worry, Mum. I'll get it.'

Jane went to the kitchen where his mother was putting things in the dish washer.

'Ah, Jane. You've been together for a while now, haven't you?' Jane felt there was a hint of disapproval in her voice.

'Yes, guess so.'

'Do you think…er…you might have…'

Martin heard her as he had come to make the coffee.

'Coffee only takes a minute, Jane, it's instant. Go back and join Dad.' Jane felt relieved and returned to the table. What was Gladys inferring to, marriage or babies?

Charles was already back in his lounge chair and she moved to the settee awaiting Martin's return with their coffee.

Half an hour later Martin decided it was time to return to Lincoln and told his parents he had work to do for tomorrow. Jane was relieved. It was clear to her that his mother wanted them to lead a more conventional life and whatever that meant she wasn't sure. Yet under the surface she felt his mother certainly wasn't one hundred percent impressed with her.

*********************

The next year was very active. Martin continued to focus on the agricultural side of his job and clearly was getting more and more business for his firm. He and Jane continued their visits to Antibes and occasionally to his little cottage in the Wolds which he rented out short term, something which Jane now looked after and had organised a local cleaner. Many customers came from London which amused her. That area with all its snuggling cottages, was a place where nature always seemed to be in control and, for her, had a kind of fairyland feel. So, so different from the place where she grew up.

She had a firm feeling that she was doing well but along with this sometimes a restlessness crept in and she started to notice the frequent times when men made it clear that they fancied her. Her relationship with Martin was becoming less about sex. She no longer teased and tempted him like the old days, although for him it continued to be a vital part of what he saw as their needs.

They were out one night in a bar, planning to go to the cinema. He put her a gin and tonic on the table and went back for his beer. She looked across at his short, more than slightly overweight body, giving a sigh and taking her first sip as he sat down next to her.

She opened the crisp packet saying,

'Are we still going to the cinema?'

'Yes. We've plenty of time.'

She held the crisp packet out towards him.

'Jane. There's something important I want to say.'

They both sipped their drinks, then he put his glass down, his face serious. 'Look at me, Jane.' She knew what he was going to say and no way did she want to hear it. She stood up immediately,

'I need to slip to the loo.'

In the well-kept toilet, she washed her hands looking at her reflection in the mirror. Makeup perfect. Not overdone. She knew what he was going to say.

He'd referred to it before and this time his seriousness disturbed her. He looked at her as she returned to the table.

'Heck, Martin. I'm looking forward to the film…'

'Yeah. Should be good.'

'Martin, no serious talk now. I've had a difficult day at work today, well, this week actually. I need to lighten up.'

She put her hand on his thigh and offered him another crisp. Gradually they ate the whole packet. Then he got up for a quick whisky and she smiled at him and shook her head, implying no more drinks for me and feeling that she was the strong one and would continue to be.

\*\*\*\*\*\*\*\*\*\*\*\*\*\*\*\*\*\*\*\*

Next day she was up and brightly sorting out breakfast. These days she rarely encouraged him for morning sex but more and more often she took charge of breakfast. As she stood beside the oven with bacon and mushrooms on the hob, she smiled thinking of the IUD she'd had fitted in her uterus, something like eight years ago. She had every intention of checking out the paperwork and wasn't sure whether it lasted forever. Vague memories seemed to be telling her she needed to get it checked and redone. Her mind flashed to one or two blokes who recently had made it clear they wanted sex with her. All such things weren't over yet but she reminded herself, as she often did these days, that she had such a financially splendid life with Martin. Recently he bought her a brand-new VW Golf with opportunity to park it in his nearby car renting garage where he already had 3 of his own cars.

\*\*\*\*\*\*\*\*\*\*\*\*\*\*\*\*\*\*\*\*

It was 3 weeks later that she knew something was coming up as they finished dinner that evening.

'Jane.' He put his wine glass down. 'Look at me.' She half knew what was coming but hoped she was wrong.

'I have to confess, though it's not really a confession. I saw your contraceptive information on your desk yesterday.'

'Ah, you mean about my IUD renewal. Why on earth did you?'

'It might surprise you, initially it surprised me but Jane, I really, really want a child.'

She reached for the wine bottle.

'I mean we've got so much to enjoy…imagine a two-year-old with us in Antibes, floating around on our pool…and come on, Jane, you'll be a lovely mother.'

She didn't reply.

'Well, think about it._Seriously I mean. You know you mean a lot to me. We could marry if you wanted and I haven't told you yet but in case I happen to die, I'll be changing my Will, leaving everything to you.'

She really didn't know what to say. The idea of his Will was intriguing.

He got up and put his hands on her shoulders. 'I'll make us a coffee.'

'No, Martin. I've got work to do, leave it for now. She got up and went to the room that had become hers since what now seemed ages ago when she'd moved all her things, with his help, from London. Now she had a computer and printer on her desk.

Next day she rang the appropriate medical centre and made an appointment to have a new IUD fitted.

# Part 3

Her job as an Estate Agent assistant was going well. Occasionally she escorted customers to look at houses but mostly she was computer based in the office. There was one other woman and she was middle-aged and did work relating to what seemed like the previous office systems when so many things were in files and folders. Some still were but not so many. So, this was Ruth and she was friendly with Jane, once inviting her to make a visit to her home in a place called Wragby. Jane hadn't done this yet but did intend to. In certain moods, she was intrigued with villages and what seemed like, well, as if she was in another country compared with the London life she knew. Surprising how many of the blokes who worked here were from villages. Occasionally, she would leave her computer and make tea or coffee for other staff members, although mostly folks made their own.

One day she was asked to take one potential customer to see a terrace house in north Lincoln. When he arrived, she introduced herself immediately feeling his eyes, as she was often aware these days, taking her in. Like when she turned away to get documents from her desk, she could still feel his 100% interest in her along with the property.

She drove him in her Golf to the area and when they got out, he stood looking at her vehicle. 'Smart, aren't they?'

'Yep, it's good. Let's get to the property, just round the corner.'

He was so tall. So handsome and she couldn't help reminding herself to focus on what the interviewer had said in her early days here. The words had stayed with her. 'It's important. What can I say? To look smart, be full of information and listen well.' They entered the house and for some reason she started to think about Martin. For whatever reason he was still being so supportive, seeming so devoted, some would say, indulging her but she was beginning to think his attitude linked up for his desire to have a child. She must stop thinking about this and concentrate on her job.

'You go and look around, I'll wait here.' She stood in the entrance area and he moved through to the kitchen.

'All very modern, updated, isn't it?' he said as he returned.

'I'll just pop upstairs.' He seemed impressed with all that, coming down to her raising his eyebrows.

'Okay?'

'I'll say.'

'Back to the office then.'

'No. You can leave me in this area and I'll have a walk around. Don't suppose you can come with me.'

'No, afraid not. But get back to us about your decision.'

'I will.' He was looking at her and smiled. She smiled in response, saying, 'You lived in Lincoln before?'

'No. Live in London…East London area.'

'Really!'

'I'm moving here to do with work.'

'Ah. I see.'

'Good place, isn't it?'

'Yes. Definitely.' She looked at her watch. 'Must go.'

She sat in her car watching him walk away up the street. Hmm…East London area indeed.

\*\*\*\*\*\*\*\*\*\*\*\*\*\*\*\*\*\*\*\*\*

Evening meal with Martin.

'Jane. I've started it.' He was pouring wine into their glasses.

'Started what?'

'You know. What I've mentioned before. All the legal stuff. My Will. When I'm dead and gone, most of it'll be yours. Properties will be in both our names.' That was good news for her but she wasn't going to show that.

'Oh, really. Heck, that's years ahead. Do you want some garlic bread?' So, he'd done it, or was doing it. Good news indeed. She'd better encourage sex tonight. She allowed herself to grin in the kitchen as she heated the bread in the oven, then she caressed his shoulder as she moved back to the table. 'And Jane…do you think you can manage the bookings for the Antibes place?'

'Know you're busy but you've done well with the Wolds cottage place.'

'Yes. I'll do it.'

'And, because my finances are doing well, I'm wondering about getting a place in London…from what they're saying I may well be getting some short-term work there and don't want to be "over-staying" with my parents.'

'I see.'

Jane struggled to take it all in, telling herself she must do and say the right things. She had some uneasy feelings about him but she didn't want to dwell on that. He was giving her so much. She must continue to feign her role as his lover, his partner.

'Coffee next,' he said, standing up as he always did. 'Let's sit on the settee.' She knew what that was all about and thought of that £25 she earned as a kid without knowing she was earning it. Then her thoughts moved on to that Food Bank: tinned spam, Heinz beans, sardines. Her mother saw that task as her daughter's responsibility and would instruct her to call in and collect after school. No other kids at school went to that food place. That bitch, her mother. Sex seen by her as an offering, receiving, selling, trading. Why didn't she get a job and earn money in what people would call, a decent way? She sighed.

'You okay, Jane? Not your periods, is it?'

'Periods. No.'

He'd never said that before.

In a half-hearted way, she later responded to his sexual needs but at the same time feeling very lucky, very lucky, very, very, lucky about being in his Will. However, if he was doing it to seduce her into having children, he was a loser.

\*\*\*\*\*\*\*\*\*\*\*\*\*\*\*\*\*\*\*\*\*

It was some months later that she came upon the guy she'd taken to see the Lincoln house. She knew he bought the house but never saw him at the times he came into the office. She was pushing her trolley around Sainsburys when a voice behind her said, 'Think I know you.'

'Oh, hi,' she said.

It flooded back. His looks and the strict business-like way she dealt with him that day.

'You shopping for your family?' he said, giving her trolley a searching look.

'Suppose you could say that.' She looked into his eyes and smiled.

'How many you got?'

'Just one.'

'Boy or girl?'

'A man.'

'Oh, sorry.'

'Have you brought all your London family to live in Lincoln?' He grinned.

'No, I've left wife and 7 children in Hackney.'

'Hackney! Hackney!'

'No er…Jane. I'm a single man.'

She was feeling entranced. Their eyes met, faces serious.

'Heck,' she said. 'I must get on.'

'Jane, you know my name, don't you?'

'Yes. Think I've still got your card.'

'Well, here's my up-to-date one.'

He lifted her hand off the trolley handle and she opened her palm. He put his card there and she closed her fingers around it before tucking it in her pocket.

He looked at her seriously and said, 'Ring me sometime… well, asap, as they say.'

'Okay. I will.'

They moved away into different aisles. She tried to focus on her shopping list but something about this bloke was intriguing her and she knew she would be contacting him.

Martin had added a whole lot of shopping to the list. What a pest he was becoming and his stomach was bulging more by the day. She came to the desserts section, recalling how her mother had been overweight but tried to slim down saying it wasn't good for business. Yes, Mother. Stupid bitch that you were, how busy you were body selling, body selling. She responded to Martin's request putting six of his favourite desserts into the trolley.

When she arrived home with her shopping, Martin was there preparing to leave the next day for London. He was doing more and more work there now and used a flat possibly in the Chelsea area or somewhere. Was it in both their names? She doubted it. Anyway, as far as she knew he was renting it. Somehow now she started wondering if he was gradually giving up the idea of a baby but then telling herself this not so. Their sex did happen but compared with early days it was certainly less frequent. For some time now, she had not been encouraging him like the old days but she always responded when he clearly wanted it. How on earth did she entice him into sex like she did in their early time together? Looking back now she had to admit to herself that she wanted to manipulate him and she did. It worked. No need to continue with that habit.

*********************

It was unbelievable. She was well into her twenties and the very thought seemed to increase the restlessness she struggled with these days. Knowing Martin was going to be 2 nights in London, she phoned Rob, asking him if he was going to stay in Lincoln.

'For time being. Yep. Hey, why don't you come and see me – you know my dwelling. I'll cook you a meal there.'

'Sounds great.'

'Any chance tomorrow?'

'You can bring your man if you like.'

'No way, he's in London at the moment.'

'Any chance tonight?'

'Every chance.'

'Seven o'clock or a bit earlier.'

'Okay. Let's say soon after 6.00.'

In preparation, she put quite a lot of thought into her appearance, deliberately going for a casual look but wanting to look appealing. She put her hair up in a coil or what her mother would have described as "a bun" with curled tresses dangling on each side. Then her new black tights with denim shorts.

Rob welcomed her, 'Hi, Jane. Looking forward to this.'

*Me too,* thought Jane. Then it was wine time and they chatted, but not seriously, about the area of London they both knew.

He knew the school she went to and she knew his, although she didn't say that. Enough was enough.

The meal he was going to cook didn't happen, as he said it was all a bit sudden, which was right. He ordered a Turkish take-away on his mobile. They chatted on about Lincoln and his work which was linked with Hull, as it involved the cargo which initially arrived there from numerous countries.

By the time they'd finished eating the food, he couldn't seem to take his eyes off her. Clearly, he was intending sex and that's exactly what she was hoping for. It happened in his bedroom. It was passionate on both sides. As she dressed later, her body was feeling so alive, so alert. He'd caressed her with such a complex mixture of assertiveness and gentleness and she became closer to orgasm than she'd ever been.

They chatted on afterwards and he made coffee as they sat up on the bed.

She drove home carefully and felt something in her life was changing. Moving on, moving on and there was a lot out there waiting.

*********************

Martin was back from London. He mentioned a visit to his parents, saying his mother would like to host another Sunday lunch. Jane nodded in agreement, feeling it was important to keep some links with his family in view of all the brewing financial issues.

Later that week when they were both back at work Jane started thinking about Rob with whom she would like more time and something in her heart was telling her that was going to happen. He rang her at work, saying how much he'd enjoyed her visit. His East London accent was there, not dominating his speech but there was a hint. She loved it. He said he'd wait to hear from her.

On a midweek night when Martin was away, she got out all the documents from his desk and was shocked to learn that his statement about changing his Will didn't seem to have happened or was it still in the process? Was he lying or were the recent documents somewhere else or did it take time to alter such vital legal documents? In anger she looked at her recent responsibility to do with rent received from short term tenants in the Wolds cottage. The last one had been three weeks and she transferred the amount to her own personal account, wondering why she hadn't done this before as Martin rarely checked their account regarding the property hiring business.

That evening Martin was there for the usual meal and wine, which Jane had become accustomed. It seemed to give her a surge of energy to deal with him; this man, this confident, dependable man who was going more and more bald by the day.

'Martin. Cheers.' She raised her glass to him. 'Aren't I supposed to have the documents about your change of Will? Guess another idea could be that I share all the properties.'

'Yes. Indeed. Haven't done it yet but will pass to you when…'

'But, you said you had done it?'

'Did I…well, I've been busy with all this work in London.' *You liar,* Jane thought, as she sipped more wine.

'Told you though, didn't I? That we're going to do another Sunday lunch with my parents? Week on Sunday.'

'Yes. Yes. Of course.' And in addition to that same day there would be time with Rob.

********************

It was a lovely autumn Sunday when they arrived together at Chelsea. His mother greeted them at the door and Jane was soon helping her in the kitchen while Martin chatted with his father about work.

'You've been together a long time now,' Gladys said as she removed the slightly boiled potatoes and transferred them to roast beside the large joint of beef. 'Hmm…'

'How's your own work going? Martin seems to be doing well with his firm.' Jane talked for a while about her work with the Estate Agent.

'Sounds you do a good job.'

'Yes, I do, but…'

'But what?'

'I'm now going to get pregnant soon. I've reached that stage…'

'You mean you're nearly thirty?'

'Yes. Well, not quite but on the way.'

'Jane, that's really good news. I'm longing for a grandchild.'

She reached over and gave Jane a kind of affectionate stroke, then adding, 'Let's go through and join "the boys" as my good friend up the road always says.'

Jane walked confidently through to the dining room, saying, 'Well done' to herself about the new replacement IUD she'd had fitted.

'Ah, put the napkins out for me, Jane.'

Jane handed round the pure while linen serviettes, something which always made her smile, well, try to smile, when she thought of growing up without such things. She'd been lucky sometimes to get food never mind all the table setting which was a natural thing here. The roast beef and Yorkshire pudding went well along with brussels sprouts and perfectly roasted potatoes. Gladys kept smiling across at Jane, who responded several times with a grin and a nod.

After a super sweet dessert, Martin made himself and Jane a coffee and they all sat in the lounge watching the golf tournament on television. Then, as usual, Martin looked at his watch saying, 'Must go, Mum. Got work re some ordered equipment for tomorrow.' His mother looked at Jane,

'Well, keep in touch,' and Jane put her thumb up as if to say, 'it'll be here soon.'

On the way home in the Rolls Royce, she couldn't stop thinking about Rob who had sent her a message this morning, 'Can't force you but need you.' His words stayed with her knowing that she felt the same about him. He made her feel like spring had come unexpectedly in a growingly dreary winter.

As he drove Martin started to talk about his mother and how she seemed to be in such a good mood.

'Perhaps because you're spending more time in London.'

'Yeah.'

'Martin, don't forget you're going to…'

'Going where?'

'Oh, leave it for now,' she spoke with impatience and picked up her mobile.

'No, Jane. You know what I mean. It's on my bucket list.'

She assumed he was referring to his Will, that Will, which she was but it seemed inappropriate to say more as heading out of London they had driven into a traffic jam. He said,

'I need to get back to Lincoln re my work.'

'Okay. I might be meeting a friend re cinema this evening.'

She sat quietly and sent text to Rob, asking if he was going to be at home this evening and his reply was immediate. 'Yes, there's a 100% chance. I'll be ready. Can't wait.'

She began to feel very alive and couldn't stop smiling as they eventually moved towards the green fields and unbuilt land. On arrival at the apartment, she immediately changed into her casual clothes and drove off in her Golf. Rob opened the door to her and welcomed her with open arms. Within minutes, they were upstairs stripping off their clothes and nestling together on the bed. Then it was sex and parts of her became so alive, her vagina moist and relaxed, and she felt nearer than she'd ever been to orgasm.

When Jane left, Rob made himself a whiskey and switched on the television.

Her suggestion that they go together to the South of France, somewhere near Nice, was appealing. There was certainly money around in her life, although she'd made it clear she didn't come from a moneyed background. He got the impression her childhood was a bit grim but she'd done well with her various jobs and now they were both on to it sexually and moving to this Lincoln area had given him a lot of pluses. His work was linking him with newly arrived cargo in Hull and its distribution. Already he'd earned more than a bit extra for handling that cannabis deal.

********************

Rob was in his car next day heading for Hull. Blurred thoughts hovered about his family. Brother and sister still alive and well, although no one knew these days where their father was. Split from his mother years ago, and she had remained devoted, committed to her offspring. His sister Rachel was still there living with her mother, although on his rare visits his mother always joked that he, her eldest son, was

50

her special one. His brother had joined the army and had remained, now stationed up in the north of the UK.

His dad. It was all a mystery. He did occasionally transfer an amount of money to their mother but that was all they knew. I was in my early teens when he stopped being around. I was just getting, what some of my school mates called the testosterone kick. Something I'm thankful for. Even now when I'm 28 that kick still thrives. I thrive. It thrives. His foot was suddenly pressing on the accelerator as he sped along on his way to Hull.

That Jane woman had referred to her bloke's Rolls Royce so there was dosh there and a place in the south of France. He was some privileged bastard that's for sure, but she, she was. He didn't need to think about it now. He was heading for the Humber Bridge and turned up his radio where Simon and Garfunkel were singing "Bridge over Troubled Waters". Bridges. Bridges. We all liked crossing them. You could never be sure what the other side would offer. It could be a fantastic change, or it might be a doom ladened finale. He smiled to himself wondering if there would be any good offers on illegal cargo today.

*********************

Time was passing. How many years since she left Tower Hamlets? Nearly four. Jane was looking across at Lincoln Cathedral. Such a magnificent building, standing there on this high area of the city and on view to all those rural areas, those wonderful fields stretching for miles, crops growing, animals amass, mostly with sufficient space to enjoy their lives. Well, sort of, as she'd learnt from Martin's talk, they were meat producers and for many their end would come. The dreaded abattoirs which Martin knew about, involved as he was with equipment for such companies. The end, the end, it happens to us all. Probably better to be a wild animal, although even then you had to look out for humans shooting you. Apparently, shoots were in abundance in that Wolds area. One of the blokes she worked with used to go and spend time with some farming relatives and, although he didn't have a rifle himself, he used to be what they called a "bush walker".

Then here too, the Norman castle. So much of it still there after hundreds and hundreds of years. She started to think about the bloke at work who had started looking into his family tree. What a waste of time! She didn't have a single relative, unlike Martin whose Uncle had left him all that stuff in his Will. She was a sole animal, like some of the rabbits here, who lost everybody they knew at the family shoots. She'd walked in the Wolds with Martin and seen the borrows rabbits made on the edges of fields. Safe places. Would she always have safe places or one day would her borrow collapse and crush her.

*********************

It was Saturday morning and Martin had gone shopping, or so he said. In fact, she'd done all the food shop. When he returned, he had several M & S bags and said he needed some new clothes. Yes, you will, Martin. Your size is on the increase. He'd been in London since Tuesday and arrived home last night when she'd gone to bed early, reading a novel but saying to him she was feeling "a bit off". What she didn't want was sex with him and her present pattern was to do all she could to play it down, although at the same time knowing that it was essential.

'Hi, Jane. You feeling better? Thought we'd go out for lunch. Been doing all this "clothes buying stuff".' He looked down at the bags.

'We're booked for 12.20.'

'Okay. I'll be ready.'

They walked to the Bull Inn and both sat peering at the menu. She looked up and noticed, as he bent down going through the choices that his hair was getting so thin and the crown part was now completely bald.

'You had a reasonable week?' he spoke as he looked around for the waiter.

'Yes. I'll have the steak one.'

'Me too,' he said looking at her raising his eyebrows.

'You're spending a lot of time in London.'

'Yes. Now I'm in the process of getting my own property there. Should be mine soon but I'm renting it now.' The waiter came and he gave their orders.

'I'm thinking of going to Antibes for an early summer holiday,' Jane said as she fiddled with her serviette.

'Well, you know if there are vacancies.'

'Yes. Already it's getting booked up.'

He didn't reply as the food had arrived but Jane continued, 'I don't always transfer the rental fees to your account because there's often money needed like the recent shower problem, not to mention the regular cleaning.'

'Jane. Listen.' She looked across at him knowing, when he started out like that, he had something serious to say. Her mind flashed to his desire for a baby.

'Yes.'

'I think or I'm sure we need to alter things. Those tasks you've been doing to do with the Wolds and France properties. I can handle all that myself now.'

'Oh, really.'

Their steak arrived. He looked across taking in her upright stature. Her back and shoulders, then thinking breasts like hers must make it hard work, but there was no evidence of that.

'So will you arrange the bookings as well?'

'Yes. I can do that, so you need to hand all the necessary information to me. Few things we might have to keep in touch about for a while.'

'Okay. Will do.' .

She wasn't sure why but, somehow, she wasn't surprised to hear this. Annoying though because her own income had increased with all this stuff. He was now immersed in his large fork full of steak. She stopped talking and didn't reply feeling for sure she would go to Antibes and take Rob.

There was no return of the closeness of those early days with Martin when she often had surges of thankfulness that he had helped her to clear out of that depressing childhood area. Get away. Get out. Now things seemed different. This man, who initially she had pondered to all his needs, no longer had her backing in the same way as their early days together. However, however, she urged herself to pay attention to his needs.

'You want a dessert?'

The waiter was waiting patiently.

'Just coffee for me.'

'I'll have two of the cream cheese...well, we'll have two and I'll share hers,' Jane said nothing but looked across at this ageing man. When the two arrived, he ate them both and didn't even ask her if she wanted a bite. Jane sipped her coffee feeling part positive, part negative, asking herself, 'where am I, where am I.'

*********************

The next day was Sunday and she was relieved to see him occupied on his computer. She rang Rob and he asked if she would like to go with him to the village where he was thinking of buying a house further north and closer to Hull. She agreed telling Martin she was meeting a friend for a shopping spree. Rob drove her to the village not far from the Humber River. Once there, he took a look at the house before deciding it wasn't for him so didn't even go inside. Jane felt relieved, feeling she needed him in Lincoln.

They drove back slowly towards Lincoln, and she found herself pouring out, what was, at times, her despairing relationship with Martin.

'Hmm.'

Rob listened but said little in response and she went on to all the troubles with financial issues saying she'd been checking all his documents but there was no trace of them now. Although some time ago he had told her he'd planned to make her inherit his properties and income if he died before her.

'All this seemed to come from his desire to have a child. Weird, he seems to have become obsessed with it. Wanting a baby. Wanting a baby.'

'Probably to do with inheritance,' Rob said, giving her a quick glance.

'Yeah. He'd always used the term "our place" when in the Wolds, in Lincoln, in Antibes, but is taking a long time to make the term "our" legal. So, it all tied to this wanting a child, wanting a child. No way, am I going down that fucking road?'

Rob didn't respond in words but kept putting his hand on her right thigh in a soothing kind of way.

The next weekend they were together in Antibes. For late spring the weather there was sunny but cool. They'd travelled down by train and Rob seemed bemused by it all.

The night before she left Lincoln Martin had said,

'I have a very good friend, a woman friend, in London. She works at the same company as me and is in the London office.'

Jane had been taken aback. Strangely she had not expected this. Not that she didn't want him to have another woman, just that it immediately brought all the financial issues floating around in her mind and an eruption of unease caused her to get up and start unscrewing the cork from another bottle of wine.

'Yes, Martin. Funny how we do make friends at work. Well, not funny really, guess it's just the way people see each other a lot.'

He didn't respond to this as he got up for his dessert, which, in his usual way he gobbled with enthusiasm.

'So, who are you going to Antibes with? You didn't say.'

'Oh. A friend from work.'

She got up and left the table, going to her study room, or that was how, these days, she described it. Recently she'd acquired a wardrobe and moved most of her clothes there, and of course, all her office type work. Things were definitely changing although they did both sleep in the same bed and sex did happen.

\*\*\*\*\*\*\*\*\*\*\*\*\*\*\*\*\*\*\*\*\*

Her week with Rob seemed like two days. It flashed by in a stimulating togetherness. Yes. Sex, sex and more. Orgasms galore, but also an easy, at times musing, friendship. He always listened to her about her life with Martin and would then grin and suggest they "move on" and enjoy their next activity in this lovely seashore French town. Could be a swim or a Picaso Gallery, or a dine out in one of the abundant choices of restaurants. 'Live for the present. Let's do that.'

He could speak a little more French than she could and seemed to be amused trying it out and sometimes failing. He also made her laugh when he switched back to a strong London accent. Then one night in the restaurant he mentioned some of the extra money he got for dealing with illegal drugs arriving at the Hull port.

'What kind of drugs?' she asked.

'Usually Marijuana, sometimes Cocaine and other times I'm not sure what it is.' I just agree to pass it on.

'Don't look worried. It's all done very secretly.' Jane smiled. This was a brave, intelligent man who knew a lot about this kind of thing. She reached across the table and touched his hand.

'Another glass?' She picked up the wine bottle and poured him one, then topped her own.

'Tomorrow's our last day here. Cheers.'

He responded, 'Cheers. Tomorrow is another day. Let's enjoy today.'

They did, and on the train going home, she took out her novel and he worked on his laptop, then said. Let's play cards. They did, and she was surprised he just took the pack out of his pocket. So, it was snap then and they both giggled.

'I've never played cards in my life,' she said.

'Well, this is a start. Surprised you didn't do this as a kid. It's a kids' game.'

*Hmm*...Jane thought. I'm not surprised.

They arrived at St Pancreas.

'Well, it's *au revoir*.'

He began to hug her and she felt her mind racing around trying to get her into her return to Lincoln mode.

'Like I said, I've got business in London before I head for Lincoln.'

********************

Ruth, at work, had said only last week. 'Are you okay, Jane? You seem a bit occupied, I mean, not with work but?'

She smiled as Ruth stood looking down at her as she sat at her desk.

'Yeah. I'm okay, Ruth. Just a few family problems.'

'Oh, I know what they can be like. You don't have children yet though?'

'No. No…'

They'd worked in this Estate Agents office for a long time now. Relatively recently she'd gone on an invite to Ruth's home in Wragby. She'd met her husband and two teenage sons and enjoyed a meal and a glass of wine with them all. The eldest one, Luke, had talked a lot with her about London and clearly was wanting to go there, perhaps live there one day. He said he couldn't wait to get out of this place, which he said was "so benign". He wanted something more alive, challenging, interesting. More mixed cultures, choice of night clubs, events. She didn't of course mention her experiences in London, and was pleased when the opportunity came to change the subject.

*********************

# Part 4

They were in Lincoln centre, sitting in McDonalds and the cafe was buzzing with customers around them. Rob looked at her in that affectionate way, his mouth closed, lips and cheeks lifted, eyebrows raised.

'You should come back with me sometime to East London, have a look. Be amused.'

'I'm not sure I would be amused.'

'You might. Never know if you don't try things out.'

She didn't reply, he added, 'I know those high rises you've told me about.'

'Well, it's one of many.'

'Hmm.'

'Your mother still living there?'

'Good heavens, no. Dead now.'

'What! Really?'

'Yes really. Died years ago when I had moved out.'

'You didn't tell me.'

'Didn't know you then, but why, why would I tell you anyway?' He was checking his watch. They were both on a lunch break.

'She wasn't a mother to regret losing. In fact, it came with some relief.' He nibbled a chip and looked at her seriously as she added.

'You liked, I mean still like your mum, don't you?'

'Yes, Yes, I guess most do.'

He sipped his coffee, adding, 'Well, she wasn't my real mum. Guess you'd say, er. what would you say?' He reached for his last bit of bacon. 'What do you mean Rob? You were adopted or something.'

'No, my dad took me to her when I was about three months.'

'Your dad…but…'

'Yeah, I think this woman, suppose you could say, my birth mother was on with a lot of blokes and my dad, well, he told me he had what was a one off with her, and later, Dad said, she told him she was pregnant, although he thought she was free of such things, as her blokes were all paying her. Her job, I guess.'

'But…'

'I asked Dad, how could she be sure that he had fathered the baby and he said she had been very definite that it was his baby. He said she'd suffered an illness soon after her sex with him and she was off work for a month, then more so as her pregnancy matured.'

'But…'

Jane looked at him with a frown.

'Seems my dad, well he did call again, and she asked him if he wanted to take me. By then, Dad was on with another woman and he said yes immediately. He'd recently married this other woman and she agreed to take me. I grew up as her eldest son.'

'Yes, you said you had a brother and sister but your dad's gone now.'

'Exactly. He has.'

They finished their meal and went back to work, agreeing that Rob would come round to her place after work. Martin was working in London.

'No more talk about babies and mothers,' he said. 'We'll just snuggle together in your apartment.'

'Okay. I'll ring you if Martin suddenly turns up but he did say he would be away until tomorrow night.'

'Perhaps I should meet him one day.'

Jane nodded but looked dubious, saying, 'Perhaps.' He laughed. 'Perhaps, perhaps, perhaps.'

*********************

Her times were changing. She recently met that young teenage son of Ruth. He had phoned her saying he wanted to talk with her about London and could they have a coffee together. She set out to meet him initially feeling she was the knowledgeable one, and that he was so, so adolescent. However, she quicky noticed that he talked with a real confidence about his various options. He could do a degree in something like History or English Literature and go on to do, the two-year course in teacher training. His parents would support him if he went this way. He would rent a place in London, probably the Greenwich area where he had a cousin, well Aunt and Uncle too. They'd let him stay with them initially until he had earnings and could rent and be independent. In the meantime, he'd have many free hours to find out about London. Apparently, according to his cousin, clubbing was in abundance.

She was thinking how sensible and carefully thought through it all was. Then he said he was getting up for the toilet. Standing behind her he put his hands on her shoulders, surprising her by kissing the top of her head. She paid for the coffees and prepared to leave. He came back to the table and said, 'Please, please can we meet again?'

'Okay. Give me a buzz.'

He did the next day, and she began to feel she was moving into a different sphere. He'd been on her mind ever since that coffee chat, although she reminded herself more than once that she had to bear Ruth in mind. Yet the idea of sex with someone as young as Luke intrigued her. He was so lythe, so face on with her, or that's how it felt. Stop it. Stop it, she told herself. Keep on that straight line, even if it was narrow, whatever that meant.

********************

She began to have lots of thoughts about what Rob had said, and the next time they met when Martin was again in London, she asked him to tell her more.

'Like where, did your birth mother live?'

'Well, Jane, that's why I asked you if you wanted a trip back to East London.'

'I see.'

'Then I'll show you where she lived.'

'Okay. Let's do it.'

'In a few weeks' time, perhaps you'll get us back to Antibes.' She laughed.

'Don't know why I'm laughing. So many things are changing. Not so easy now about Antibes, as Martin's handling the bookings.,

'Oh, really!'

'Yes but I could say you're a friend from work. I said that before.'

'Well, that's exactly what I am.'

Rob looked at her opening wide those blue eyes, and then grinning.

'Don't forget, I could take you to meet my mum sometime if you fancied it.'

'What! Well, perhaps.'

'Perhaps, perhaps, perhaps.'

They both laughed and turned back to the menu.

*********************

In the meantime, she met Luke again. He had arranged to meet her at this flat on Monks Road. It was where one of his friends lived but was away for a week on something to do with his recent business job. She'd never been to that part of Lincoln and walked there. Arriving half an hour late she tapped on the door and he was there, all ready and waiting. On her arrival, he cooked her scrambled egg on toast with a glass of wine. All very enjoyable after a day at work. Then he came round to her side of the table and started to stroke her.

'Luke, I'm not sure about all this touching.'

'Why not. I love touching you.'

She started to lose that sense of being careful, standing up beside him.

'Touch me, Jane, touch me.'

She did and he pulled his trousers down revealing a lovely pair of boxer shorts and she could see his bulge was on the increase. She stripped off her jeans and pants and they fell together on the settee. He seemed a bit unsure about penetrating her and she guided him in the right direction, feeling a strong urge now to get him inside her, but he soon seemed to be losing his erection and she caressed him and gradually decided it was better to leave it there. 'It takes time, Luke, but It's lovely to see you. I need to go soon. I've got a partner you know. Perhaps shouldn't be doing this.'

'Yeah, well.' He hesitated. 'We will see each other again, won't we?'

'Well, Luke, I'll have to think about it. You know I work with your mother, don't you?'

'What's that got to do with it?'

She didn't respond and reached for her jeans.

'I'll make you a coffee.' He stood up pulling on his pants.

'Okay, but, as I said, I need to go soon.'

She withdrew from her desire to have sex and talked to him in a counselling way about whether he'd had sex with any other women, and he said he hadn't, not yet. One girl his age had tried to talk him into it but somehow his thoughts were on getting out of Lincoln and he'd avoided her.

\*\*\*\*\*\*\*\*\*\*\*\*\*\*\*\*\*\*\*\*

A few weeks passed by, and Martin was now staying for longer periods in his London place and seemed to be seeing his parents more often. In his absence, she invited Rob over a couple of times and felt pleasure in having him sleep beside her in the double bed. Meanwhile Martin kept taking more and more of his belongings to his London place and had still not suggested she see his initially rented apartment in Knightsbridge or wherever it was. She wasn't knowledgeable about that area of London. He returned one day and said, 'I'm going back later today.'

'Oh.'

'I've got this woman from the office moving in with me.'

'Oh. Moving in with you?'

'You can stay here for the time being. I'll talk more about it later.' 'I see.'

It wasn't that she cared about him and another woman, it was the financial situation which was vitally important to her, and his comment about being able to stay here for the time being alarmed her. Whatever did that mean?

'There is talk of marriage.' That was it then. That was it.

'Really. Has she met your mother?'

'Yes. They get on well. So, I'm heading back today as she needs help moving.'

When he'd gone, Jane fished around for his documents but there was no trace of anything to do with his financial plans. He'd already taken all such documents with him.

Talk of marriage. Talk of marriage. Of course, all this meant he'd change his Will. So, all that she thought would one day be hers wasn't. Or was it? His Will, his Will. Did she have any legal strength in all this? Could she take legal action for at least half of so many of his properties. She doubted it.

She began to feel more and more angry. How could this fat old man decide to leave her? No babies. No babies. How dare he think that was more important than continuing their relationship? Why did it all start to become a prime need? No way was she having children. Didn't even want to think about it now. Children. Childhood. Childhood. Not for me. Not for me.

Rob came on Sunday and stayed over before dashing off to Hull re. work. They had become such good friends as well as lovers. He had changed things. All these years, starting off with that unforgettable childhood sexual experience, when she was only eleven years old. It had put her off enjoying sex but using it for the various positives that came from men. In Martin's case all the initial assets. Now at last she was experiencing orgasms. With Rob. With Rob.

On her way to work, she received a message from Martin saying he was planning to marry Maria. So, what would happen with all the legal stuff she had with him? The Will. The Will. Er. She wasn't sure.

It was becoming clear to Jane that there was no Joint Partnership ever legalised, although he had frequently implied that this had been done or was being done. Of cause, had it really happened, she would have been given her own copy for signing and agreeing. There had been no signing on her part. So, there was just his Will, in which he'd recently showed her, three quarters of his finances would go to her on his death and the rest to his parents although, he said it was unlikely he'd die before them.

She discussed all this with Rob, who came round that day immediately Martin left for Knightsbridge.

'Yes. The thing about Wills, I guess, you can change them. If he, say gets married. From your point of view, it's all a bit dodgy now.'

'Hmm.'

'Together we'll sort it.'

'God knows how.' But perhaps he does, Jane thought as she looked across at Rob, her mouth tightened. Her fury about Martin's plans kept boiling inside her, her wish being to strike him, kick him, batter him, burn him. Something about it all reminded her of that mother, that awful woman, using her on several occasions to odd ones of her clients wanting a younger body. She'd got away, moved out of that hole, that brothel, leaving that, that allegedly mother person, and found a place to share with two other young girls. She was 16 then and worked in what was a sort of assistant to assistants in various offices. It had felt like an escape, and her will to be a good employee got stronger. There were other ways of earning money and initially her first fortnightly salary, meagre as it was, at the time gave her bursts of satisfaction. Her approach to men at work became very formal, polite, exactly how it was supposed to do in business. She'd succeeded, she'd succeeded.

Her father, her father. She never knew who he was, and it was likely that he was one of her mother's customers, and that brothel-living creature never knew which one.

Now, when she looked back over her many years with Martin, she wondered what on earth was she doing. Selling herself. Making money. Pondering to him and living in what she saw as a privileged life. It had all seemed okay in those early years, new area, new job, and looking back now she had thought, on the odd occasion, he was like the father she never had, never knew. Then gradually, gradually, her resentment towards this man had started to build up.

Then there was all that business about him wanting a child, along with his mother, and he was well into his fifties now. All these thoughts dominated her, and more and more often she began to feel on the low side.

Now here she was again with Rob, her thoughts oddly occupied. She turned to look at him, her first real male friend, the one who had given her so much, not just sexually, but he'd listened to her, often showing empathy.

'Jane, you're getting depressed. Might be a good idea to have a bit of my unlicensed sniff and we could go down to London at the weekend.'

Initially she had no idea what he meant about his sniff but focussed on him wanting to take her to London. 'Yes. Let's go on Saturday.'

He got her to relax and showed her how to sniff cocaine, something she'd never done but was amazed how strong and positive it made her feel. They laughed a lot and he eventually stayed with her overnight, saying he had to leave early as his work next day would be in Hull.

Next morning when she awoke her resentment towards Martin seemed to be increasing, dominating her mood. It was only when Rob stirred and put his arms around her that all such feelings fell away. As he began to touch her, sex became imminent and for those moments made her forget everything.

********************

Saturday came and Rob picked her up. They headed for London and she tried to be amused. They eventually drove through the high-rise areas virtually passing through her birthplace. Then he drove on into an underground car park. They got out, using a lift to get up to the 10$^{th}$ floor level. His mother was expecting them and greeted Jane in a warm way, before making them cups of tea and offers of a chocolate cake.

Jane accepted the offer and enjoyed the cake. Elsie said, 'I made it myself.'

'Oh, really?'

'Well, he is my...' she hesitated, looking at Rob, 'my important son.'

'Yeah. He's been a good friend to me.'

'He said you came from this area.'

'Yes. I did.'

'It has its assets, you know. Full of character this area and it's easy to use public transport to get around.'

'And, Mum, Jane grew up in Longworth Street.'

'Oh, did you? You know about it all then. When did you leave?'

'Er, over 5 years ago now. Haven't been back.'

'And your mother?'

'She died when I was 16.'

Elsie said no more and talked to Rob about his brother who was doing well up North, in the army, and had been made a corporal.

'Would you believe that?'

'Yes, I would, Mum. He's always been committed and my sister. Still living here, is she?'

'Yes. Doing well in Marks and Spencer's. Assistant to the manager in the Lingerie Department.'

'What do you do, Jane?'

'Oh, I work in an Estate Agents office.'

'Oh, yes, Rob told me that was how he met you.'

'Well, Mum, we must get off. I'm going to drive Jane to the street where she grew up. Never been back since she left all that time ago.'

'Yes. Go and have a look. It's good to see you both and come again.'

'We will, Mum. I certainly will.'

As they left the flat and headed along the corridor to the lift, Rob said, 'Interesting, isn't it. Mum's happy enough here.'

They left the car in the underground car park and walked out to the street. Rob had checked and knew exactly where Jane's high-rise was. She was very quiet and kept eyeing up the buildings.

'Here we are, Longworth Street. Short and sweet, isn't it?'

Jane noted the street. Yes, it was short but not sweet, each end moving into a long busy road.

'Yes, I see it. It hasn't changed much.' She was far from delighted and hoped Rob didn't want to take her to level nineteen.

'Yep. Well, I wasn't expecting you to be delighted but it's good for you to see it. It's real, isn't it?'

She turned and looked at Rob, then said, 'Perhaps, perhaps, perhaps.' They laughed and he led her back to the car park, and she felt relieved as he drove out.

They stopped for lunch on the way back to Lincoln.

*********************

She tried to focus on herself, searching for bits she admired, like her life in Lincoln, all the good things she had done, not perfect but good, her success at work, her self-discipline, her determination to cope with Martin except for him wanting a child and, in that respect, she was right not to respond to his desire.

71

She'd done the right thing there and that's what life is like. Things complicate things. However, now a lot was changing, and she had to face the fact that she was moving into new areas.

When she was at work next day, she got a phone call from Luke, 'Hi, Jane. I want to meet you again. It's all clear on Monks Road. I'm hoping we can do that again.'

'Well.'

'Well what?'

'Okay, let's do it.'

'Great, Jane. Is Thursday okay for you? Early evening. I'll get a bottle of Rose.'

'Don't worry about that, Luke. I'll bring a bottle.'

'Okay. Great. See you there at 6:30.'

Jane looked across at Ruth who had bustled over to collect files from a shelf near her desk.

'Hi, Jane. How's things?'

'Not too bad.' She grinned and thought, *I'm meeting your lovely son on Thursday, don't think that would get me any approval.*

'And you. Everything all right in Wragby?'

'Not too bad, although Luke is driving us up the wall. He needs to get the offer of university in London accepted. Keeps putting it off.' Jane didn't respond, and Ruth continued.

'Wait 'til you have kids that age. They aren't good at making decisions. Keep changing their minds.'

'Yeah, I can imagine. Think I was a bit like that.'

So, Thursday came, and they did meet up in that little flat on Monks Road. It was a charming place, the apartment developed as an extension to an old Victorian building, opposite the Arboretum Park. She hadn't noticed all this on her last visit. He opened the bottle of wine she'd handed to him and gestured for her to sit at the table as he poured them a glass full each.

'Hi, Luke. How's your London plans going?'

'Yeah, I'm still hovering a bit.'

'Still working at the butchers?'

'Yeah, but not sure how long.'

They clinked their glasses and said the usual "cheers".

Then he stood up and moved to stand behind her, hands on her shoulders.

'You really are a sexy woman.'

She moved her face round to him, surprisingly feeling sexually stirred by his comment.

'Exciting for you, is it?'

'Well, yeah. I fancy you. Think about you a lot. Pull myself off, again and again.'

'Ah, and here we are. Let's live for the present.' She stands up beside him and reaches around his backside, his buttocks seeming so young, so beautifully shaped. Then they are on the settee again and he is ripping off his boxer shorts, before pulling off her pants. She is craving for him now and he penetrates with success. She feels her orgasm is coming but it doesn't quite make it as he ejaculates into her and withdraws.

'Thank you, Jane. Thankyou.' He can't stop saying it. Jane sits up gathering her clothes, wondering if she should say something about her experience, then decides not to, well not on this occasion.

They finish drinking the bottle of Rose, and he offers her a bag of crisps. She eventually says her goodbye, and Luke looks at her, trying to get her full attention.

'I want to see you again, Jane, and soon.'

'Okay. Give me a buzz.'

She walks away, knowing that Martin will be there when she gets home. She crossed the Arboretum Park area feeling, for some reason, captivated by the beautifully organised gardens, lawns, trees and shrubs. What is it about nature, so controlled in areas like this, whereas in parts out there in the country she sometimes wasn't sure what nature was up to. Some spots seemed to be running rampant, unlike others which were being controlled by the process of farming. She looked at the pond where the ducks were happily swimming around, seeming to enjoy each other's company.

She arrived home feeling she needed to see Rob but knowing he was working in Hull for a few days. She told herself not to clash with Martin. There was no point. However, the apartment was empty when she arrived home. She decided to make herself an omelette and have a few more sips of wine. Halfway way through all this she got a phone call from Martin. He'd decided to stay overnight in London but might head for Lincoln tomorrow.

'Jane. I'm happy for you to keep your car?'

'Okay.' What on earth was that about. Of course, it was her car. Given to her as a gift, and you can't take gifts away. 'See you tomorrow.'

'Yep.'

So that was how everything was now. She knew but it was still discomforting, and she started sipping from one of Martin's whisky bottles.

Friday morning and she was at work but feeling a bit on the drowsy side after all that whisky last night. She put on a very bright persona and joked with one of the agents about somebody wanting a house in a village called Apley. 'They've got a lot to spend,' he said.

'They're wondering about a manor house, or a Hall, something large and grand but perhaps in an isolated area. Nothing like that available in Apley but I'm looking at other areas.'

When she was making herself a strong coffee in the kitchen area, as they called it, Ruth came up to her.

'Jane. I need to talk to you privately. Can we just meet at M and S coffee place after work?'

'Can't do it today, Ruth. Got serious things going on at home.'

'Oh, well. Leave it for now.'

Back in the office she immersed herself in work, partly trying now to wonder what Ruth's request was all about, but, of course, knowing it.

********************

She was due for another week's leave from work, and when Martin had sent that message, saying that his marriage was now planned and he needed to make a final visit, she'd decided to take the leave. Rob also arranged some time off work saying he would be there when "that bloke" came.

Jane knew that the Will would be changed after this bitch, Maria, married him. In fact, he's probably already done this, and the document will go into operation on the marriage date. Fuck. Fuck. What a fat old traitor he'd become.

Rob left early for work next morning and she was feeling unusually sleepy.

He whispered,

'Don't rush to get up. You've loads of time before work.' Then she heard the door close and lock.

She settled back beneath the duvet before deciding to take a few more sniffs of, whatever…and then got up to ring the office to confirm this one week's leave and wanting it to start today. Gerald answered and said it would be okay although usually weeks off are planned earlier. 'We'll manage, although we need a woman like you dashing around.'

'Thanks, Gerald.' She put the phone down and thought over what she heard in the office, only last week. Gerald had talked on about something called Strychnine – well she'd had to look that word up. Apparently, it is a pesticide that kills rats, and his family had been struggling for ages with what he called, the rodent devils. It was a kind of powder which had worked well.

Rodent devil. Rat. Rat. Why don't I get some? She reached out to the wonderful product that Rob had shared with her. What was it? Cocaine? Never had she had anything like this before.

********************

Later that day she had another message from Martin confirming he'd be here tomorrow, and this would be his final visit. He arrived in the morning and the first thing he said as he looked around making sure he'd got everything, 'Yes, Jane. You can have another month here and then it's either rent or leave. Choice is yours.' It felt unreal. Why was this happening?

He started to look around the place for the few possessions he hadn't yet taken. There was a computer which he carried out saying,

'I'm going to have to change vehicles. I'll take the Jaguar into the garage and bring the Land Rover out for all this stuff.'

'Thankyou.' Everything seemed so complex. It was then that Rob arrived and greeted Martin with a handshake. Martin seemed a bit surprised. Jane glanced at this short, overweight, ageing man and the handsome, tall, young one with the bluest eyes she'd ever seen. Rob looked at her and grinned. Martin dashed off to change his vehicle and when he returned Rob gave him a friendly touch on the arm and started to talk to him about London. Martin responded and said a lot about Lincoln and his job with agricultural implements, tractors, trailers, all stuff to do with harvesting, ploughing, sowing. He went on to tell his links with other businesses to get crew yards and barns built.

'Must have been a useful spot for you living here,' Rob said.

'Yes. Indeed.'

Martin turned to Jane. 'As I said, I'm leaving the Jaguar here. Need to use the Land Rover to get back to London with all the stuff. Not as much as I expected but just brought it back and left the Jaguar temporarily. You'll soon have to move your Golf? I've sold that parking building. It's going to be demolished and houses built.'

She didn't answer but could see Rob was paying attention. That was what she wanted.

'And, Jane. I'm marrying Maria on 15th.' The word 15th rolled around in her mind and wasn't going to leave.

'Martin.' She looked down at her watch. 'Rob's ordered all three of us a takeaway lunch. Due in a minute.'

They all sat around enjoying a mozzarella pizza, salad and garlic bread. 'Well, I'd better get on with it,' Martin said. 'Need to get back asap.'

'I'll get us a coffee,' Jane said.

She went into the kitchen and looked at the rat poisoning inside the small, lidded pot she'd brought here years ago when she moved from the rented flat in East London. Rodent rat. Rodent devil. She looked out of the kitchen window towards the cathedral.

She could hear Martin going on about his work and his liking for, was it Knightsbridge? We all need to move, he kept saying. Change can be a good thing, and then criticising his parents who are in the same house they moved into after marrying.

Then Rob came into the kitchen.

'I'm just coming, Rob. Sounds he's going on a bit.'

'I'll open.'

'The what?' Her thoughts were elsewhere. He took it out of the fridge and began to open it.

'The champagne. Thought we should celebrate.'

'Oh, I don't think I can do it.'

'What?'

'Not the champagne, my plan. You know.'

'Jane. He's popped out to speak to the garage bloke again. Tell you what, have a sniff of this.' She did it more than once. Then she opened the pot and showed Rob what was inside, thinking, *I'll do it. I'll do it.*

'Jane,' Martin shouted. 'I've talked to the garage chap. Need to get off now.' She walked into the dining room.

'Like I said perhaps you'll drive it back to me, the Jaguar, and come back here on the train.' He returned to the table to briefly eat what was left of the cheese and biscuits.

Rob walked in with three glasses of champagne on a tray, putting one in front of Martin. Then it was "cheers" and they all sipped.

Martin got up quickly after his glass raising, and as Jane and Rob continued to sip their champagne he said,

'Right. I'm off.'

'Sure, you've got everything,' Jane said.

'I'll leave the Jaguar keys here for when you have time to drive it back.' He almost banged them down onto the table before reaching out picking up his champagne and slurping the drop remaining.

'Bye.'

He didn't even look at them, seemed only now occupied with wanting to get back to London.

She watched from the window as he drove off, thinking *Goodbye, goodbye.* All over and done.

'Can I stay over?' Rob said.

'Certainly.' She moved over to him and put her arms around him. They embraced, both feeling a bit bewildered.

'So, he's leaving you your Golf?'

'Of course. That was a gift.'

'Hmm.'

'No really.'

'Well, we'll see how it all goes,' he uttered, as he began to search for her lips, and they kissed for a long time before making their way to her bed.

\*\*\*\*\*\*\*\*\*\*\*\*\*\*\*\*\*\*\*\*\*

A few days later she was informed of Martin's death. His mother said he had died on his way back from Lincoln. He crashed his car on the M1 motorway. 'Think the funeral will be on the 12th.'

Gladys added, 'I'll let you know. Think his new woman will be there.' The irony was his funeral would be just a few days before his planned wedding, although Gladys didn't say that.

Jane had looked into her secret little pot and found half of the powder had vanished. Even before she looked, she knew. Did she, do it? Her memory was muzzled. One moment she thought she didn't, next moment sure that she did. She sniffed her last portion of the cocaine and thought, *Nothing mattered.* He was gone. He deserved it. Her life looking good. The Will, the Will. Hopefully. Hopefully.

She decided she would go to the funeral and asked Rob if he would go with her, but he declined, saying he'd look forward to seeing her on return.

She was at work next day, but felt a bit uneasy, about the funeral. Go or don't go. She'd implied to his mother that she would go. Only Rob consoled her when he returned after work. More sniffing together, more sex. Luke rang saying he'd love another meeting on Monks Road, but she explained that, at the moment, she was busy with family things. That very afternoon Ruth approached her saying,

'I need to talk to you. We'll talk outside where you know I pop out and have my smoke thing.'

'I'm busy but I'll come by 11.30.'

When she got outside, Ruth was waiting.

'Jane. I'm annoyed with you. You know why, don't you?

'You mean.'

'Yes. I mean, Luke, my son. Please, stop seeing him.'

'Well, he wanted to talk about London and he's thinking seriously about going there.'

'Yes. To university we hope.'

There was a pause and Ruth took an intake of her cigarette thing.

'I don't trust you, Jane. You're an attractive woman, even some of the blokes here joke about that. If Luke starts fancying you, that's trouble. He's got to get away, Jane.'

Jane shuffled uneasily.

'Okay Ruth. I promise I'll keep my distance. Can I go in now? I've got work. Am going to London on Monday for a funeral. Got time off.'

'Well, don't forget.'

'Okay.' *I'll try,* Jane thought, as she headed back to her desk.

Back in the office that lovely villa in Antibes flashed into her mind. She should go with Rob again. Such thoughts cheered her up and she grinned thinking perhaps, perhaps, perhaps.

# Finale

She was often preoccupied with thoughts about the funeral, amazing really that she even went, and driving back in that Jaguar. Not what you asked for Martin but one doesn't always get what one asks for. The Will, the Will. I won't be getting a penny of that now. Such thoughts would make her stand up and pace around her tiny white painted cell, often looking out of the small, narrow barred window, watching some prisoners doing their morning walks in the big yard surrounded by high walls topped with barbed wire. It all brought back the same old memories, her life in that high rise place, her childhood, her mother doing what no one else's mother did. Odd that period of her life was always there, so many aspects of it not forgotten, living on, especially when she was alone as she was now. Yet many memories of later times seem to be sliding away.

Apparently, the police, at the funeral time, had initially been uncertain about what the poison was and the forensics were still working on it. She'd destroyed anything that might have assisted their scrutinising. That little pot of hers, she had bleached it and then decided that wasn't enough and smashed it taking pieces out and throwing them away in different places, then deleting all the stuff on her computer when she had ordered the rat killer. Yes, she thought she had, but it was likely, from what was said in court, that some of it was retrieved.

Strangely, as initially when she'd looked into the Strychnine information, she'd found there had been a woman in Lincolnshire in the 1930's who had put this poison in her husband's corned beef bread sandwich. He had become ill and died the next day. Eventually she was accused in court of killing him and the guilty verdict was finally made. In those days, a woman killing her husband this way, even if he had treated her violently for many years, putting poison in his food was seen as unforgivable. Whereas beating him with a fireplace poker was considered a little more reasonable. Ethel Lillie Major was hanged in Hull prison 19th December 1934. It was the last of ten hangings and the only female execution at Hull. At the time she'd told Rob and he'd made jokes about Hull, saying he'd look around for the prison next time he was working there adding, 'Most people don't have any idea what goes on in that place,' winking at her and making her share a bit more of his cocaine.

Now Jane was thinking she would prefer to be hanged rather than spending the rest of her life being shut up here. Did she put that stuff in his champagne? Was it her? Was it her? Or was it him. He knew the power of that cocaine sniff. Nevertheless, that fat little man had to go, and he was gone. But now, all to no avail.

She remembered Martin leaving that afternoon, and Rob had seemed to applaud her actions, vague as she was herself. He remained confident about how it would all turn out and made jokes about, why didn't she start learning French. They could move to live in Antibes.

She recalls often the funeral and his father standing up saying, 'I'm afraid I have something very serious to announce.' She'd left immediately knowing it was an issue she didn't want to hear about. Apparently, there was no burial that day and the body was taken back to the forensics who, within two days, discovered the dreaded, er what was it, beginning with "S" word, the rat poisoning. Martin's father had kept close contact with the police. He would, wouldn't he. Legal chap that he was. The day the rat stuff was discovered the police arrived at her place asking many questions.

It did all occupy her, and she became nervous, welcoming that gift of cocaine Rob had left. When Luke rang her, she put on an appearance of being busy with family things although for the next week she'd continued her work at the Estate Agents avoiding any contact with Ruth. She had no news about the Will. Then in nine days after the funeral the police had turned up again and she was nabbed, arrested and confined in a Lincoln prison.

A week later she had a letter from Luke.

*Dear, Jane, I don't believe you did it. You've been in all the local papers and television showing you being led from court into that prison vehicle and cameras all over. My mother said she didn't think you did it and said some other people where you worked were doubtful. Take care. Can't wait to meet you again, Jane. XX Luke*

When Rob visited her in the Lincoln prison, Jane was feeling totally confused. This was something she'd never thought about, being arrested, imprisoned. She should have realised this could happen, but her mind had been focussed elsewhere and her confidence about a beneficial outcome had been, well what some would say a little, or more than a little, over-confident.

'Hi, Jane. Your trial's coming up. You're going to get off, I'm sure.'

'Well, I admire your confidence. Not sure now whether I will.'

'I've bought you this book on the French language. It got through the test at the prison entrance just now and I was allowed to bring it for you.'

She took the book, knowing what it was all about. Trying to encourage her to happy thoughts and memories about their trip there. She tried to be appreciative and Rob grinned, saying,

'Perhaps, perhaps, perhaps.'

Unfortunately, she couldn't smile. She looked down at the table, moving her eyes away from the book.

'I went to see my mum again at the weekend. Drove back past your high-rise place.'

She didn't answer and he looked across at her, thinking she must be the most attractive prisoner they'd ever had here, then adding,

'Can't help wondering if my dad did go back to my birth mother er. Say about 2 years later.'

Jane looked across at the prison officer, thinking she didn't want to hear any more about this birth mother, as he called her. If he was a brother, or a half-brother, it destroyed so much of her initial feelings about their sex together, the physical delight, the satisfaction, the sense of at last finding the neglected parts of her own body.

'Jane. It doesn't matter. Makes no difference to anything. What we really want is to get you out of here and I'm sure we will.'

The prison officer came up looking at his watch, indicating their time was up.

They both stood up. 'Bye, Rob. Thanks for coming.' He grinned.

'You're more than welcome.' Then it was back to her cell.

Her trial came up quickly and lasted 5 weeks. Initially she denied the charges. The poison had been identified, but there was no proof of who had given it to him, although it was, according to the police ninety percent likely that she had included it in that final meal. Then proof on her internet was somehow retrieved about her involvement with the strychnine poison. Martin's father was always in court, and she tried to avoid eye contact with him. Then the verdict came, and she was found guilty, but prior to the jury returning after their long break, she had decided what to do. She was going to admit she did the poisoning, so when the answer from the jury was 'Guilty,' *Quite right,* she thought, she did it, she did it, even if she didn't, and she was led back to her cell, before being transported to a London prison.

\*\*\*\*\*\*\*\*\*\*\*\*\*\*\*\*\*\*\*\*

Sometimes she thought of that Chelsea home and the way Martin's parents, especially his mother, would now be consoling Maria, whose pregnancy would be continuing. To become a grandparent would be Gladys's delight. Losing Martin wouldn't have affected her, as it would some mothers, so long as this pregnancy continued.

In her cell, Jane feels she has given everything up, but then she didn't have anything. No father, no mother, she was orphanlike, and the unforgettable days of men turning up in that high rise flat, it was so small and when you looked out of the windows all you could see was more high, towering buildings. Back came the images seeming to flood back in the usual way. Now she was confined, restricted, all of which seemed to click with those days. Then the money she got that day. Wow! What an achievement. Yes, or no. She was never sure, and it happened a few more times, before starting to feel bad. All bad. Almost all bad. All these thoughts now made her feel sick, and she could feel the vomit coming up, as she moved to the sink in her cell, then back again to lie on the bed.

Toilet, sink, bed, table. That was about it. Now her meals were being brought to her cell, but she knew there was a more general area where some prisoners joined a room to eat. Breakfast: egg and bread, no butter. Lunch: always seemed to be stew, and evening meal: a mug of tea and thick bread sandwich that you waited for wondering what would be in that sandwich today, cheese, sardines, spam. She'd been given A4 paper, a notebook and 2 pencils, 1 biro. So far, she hadn't written a word.

Then, after four weeks, she was allowed a visitor, and the obvious person came to see her. It was him. Was she here, or should it be him? She sat waiting for him in a guarded room, at a small table with 2 chairs. One or two other prisoners were waiting. Rob came,

'Hi there,' he said, looking at her across the table with those blue eyes.

'Good to see you,' she said, wondering whether she meant that.

'Latest news is that the Maria woman has a son. He's going to be called Martin. It's all been in the local paper.'

'Hmm…I suppose all that stuff has been.'

'Yes, it was…time you moved to London prison. There was a lovely photo of you in The Sun.'

Jane felt muddled, in one way, bursts of pleasure in seeing Rob, but then bursts of not wanting to see him. She tried to bring a smile to her face, but it wouldn't come. Her lips tightened.

'How's it been with you?'

'Me. Okay I suppose. In a way.' He raised his eyebrows. 'I've moved to live in a place near Hull. Jane. You haven't forgotten what I told you about my mother, have you?'

'Your mother?'

'Yes, what she told me about my birth mother.'

'Oh.'

'Told you when you were in the police security room before your trial.'

'Not sure that I heard anything that day.'

'Jane, my mother was pretty certain that my birth mother was your mother.' Today Jane found this absurd but didn't show it.

'If that's right, sounds like you were lucky indeed.'

'But you know it means I'm your half-brother.'

'My half-brother.' She looked at his blue eyes. Surely not. They couldn't be. Yet it was very possible. Half-siblings.

Pause

'Nothing matters now, does it?'

'Jane. Are you wondering how my mother knew this?'

'Err.'

'Well, she was fond of my dad. My dad, even though he kind of disappeared when I was in my early teens. She described to me how I was born to this woman, saying it was an accident on her part and my father had paid for sex, never thinking this pregnancy would occur. He went back to see her again many months later and she told him she had just given birth but didn't want the baby. What should she do?'

Jane didn't seem to feel the shock he was expecting.

'So that was me, Jane.'

'Oh. Guess that was all before me. Sounds like that bitch didn't have safe contraception.'

'Yeah, most likely.'

They didn't speak for a while and Jane put her hand up looking at one of the prison officers, then shouting,

'Could I have some water?'

The officer looked across at another officer who went out and popped back with a mug of water.

'Well, apparently when my dad went back to your mother's, sometime later, she was trying to get back to business. She thought he wanted sex but he said a definite no, saying he wanted to take the baby. He had a partner now and she would be a good mother, in fact when he'd discussed it with this partner, she had been adamant that she would love to take full care of the baby.' Jane sipped her water. Half wanting to hear no more, but her other half thinking they should have whatever the tests were, they should find out for certain. What if they had the same father? He might have gone back to see this bitch two years later, and then me, me.

'Jane. You okay?'

Her tone was icy, her lips tightened.

'Is that what I'm supposed to be?'

89

He didn't answer immediately, and she got up quickly. An officer came over and walked with her to the door and all she felt was that she was going back to her cell, her life spot.

Rob got up, looking a bit startled and shouted, 'Bye. See you again.' She didn't reply and thought it unlikely.

\*\*\*\*\*\*\*\*\*\*\*\*\*\*\*\*\*\*\*\*

Back in her cell she threw herself down on the narrow bed, staring up at the white, more than white coloured ceiling. Seeing Rob. Seeing Rob. He was a good friend. Friend. Friend. Not to mention all the other stuff. She'd found it. After many years, she knew now about orgasm. Never any chance with that fat old bloke. Thankyou Rob. Thankyou. Trouble was, she was sure now that he was the one who put the dreaded drug in Martin's glass of champagne. In court, she'd never mentioned how he'd collaborated with her, not to mention he was finally the guilty one. She had no regrets though. It was what she intended, what she wanted, and it worked. Well, it worked but didn't work. Not a penny, not a single penny from that Will. She ruffled her hair and turned onto her tummy, giving short sharp breaths, before getting up and going over to the sink and vomiting this morning's breakfast, then taking the biro and A4 paper over to her bed.

\*\*\*\*\*\*\*\*\*\*\*\*\*\*\*\*\*\*\*\*

*Dear Rob,*

*I thought when I found you, I'd found the pearl in my oyster. Now it seems like I've made another mistake. You're not my pearl, you're my brother. I'm sure if we had checks on our DNA, it would all be revealed. Of that I'm certain.*

*I reckon your father came back for a quick visit to our mother and she was still struggling with contraception. She always told me what an awful mistake I was. She never wanted me and didn't work for almost a year or more during my birth period. Somehow that woman seemed to blame me for all this, and regarded me as a total nuisance and I grew up living with all that, seeing myself as well below everyone else, along with owing something to her. Yet I did well at school and shouldn't have left before any exams.*

*Well, perhaps I'm wrong about our fathering. Perhaps, perhaps, perhaps.*

*I wish you all the best when I have gone.*

*Amen*
*Jane*

*Dear Luke,*

*I'm back in London now. In prison. Suppose you've heard about all this. Guilty of murder, so they say.*

*It's not the best place to be in London. I'm sure there are many, many other options which you will enjoy. No more time together for us. Just get on with accepting your university booking. You'll then find all the other delights in this city.*

*Give my regards to your mother.*

*Amen*
*Jane*

\*\*\*\*\*\*\*\*\*\*\*\*\*\*\*\*\*\*\*\*

The next morning, when the cells were being checked, Jane was found dead on the bed. She had strangled herself with a small wet towel, one of which was in every cell.

# Story 1: Resolute

Charlie had grown up here on this farm in Lincolnshire. Best land in the country, his father said, and his grandfather, and no doubt his great grandfather. His one and only sister was older than him and she had gradually started to do more work in her homeland. Now she could drive a tractor and helped her mother indoors with various jobs. Not just cleaning and washing clothes but making pork sausages and stuffing when they killed a pig. Even as a little girl she had helped her mother plucking pheasants and partridges which grandpa, who died some years ago, used to kill at regular shoots.

He didn't like this assuming, this attitude that he would be working here when next term he would be leaving school. The farm workers always treated him as if he was going to be their boss. One elderly one of them used to doff his cap, partly teasing but friendly, respectful, and when he'd grinned in confusion, he would do it again. Any others around saw it as a joke, quietly grinning and moving off to focus on their various jobs.

\*\*\*\*\*\*\*\*\*\*\*\*\*\*\*\*\*\*\*\*

At 18, Charlie was waiting for his A Level results and got himself a job in Butlins as a Redcoat when the summer holidays started. His dad reckoned he should do agriculture like there was a local college, or these days, he said some universities now did this. However, when at Butlins his results were brought to him by his mother. She was in tears about the outcome, but Charlie didn't care. By then, he was linking up with a gorgeous Redcoat woman and his sexual life was aglow. 'Don't worry, Mum. I'm still going to do well.'

Summer ended and he moved to London where Emma had accommodation in a bedsit. She was quickly back to work using all her office skills and swimming regularly as she did in her Redcoat days.

*********************

'So where am I?' he asked himself. He wasn't sure but wasn't going back to the farm. Emma's bedsit meant they had to share the bathroom, toilet and kitchen with other residents. After a few months, it began to feel a bit on the overcrowded side. Like when you were in the bathroom there was always someone knocking on the door, needing, he assumed, the toilet, or a quick shower prior to leaving for work, or cleaning up after a lonesome, messy, masturbation.

He got a job in a local fruit and veg shop and started to do a carpentry course in the local college. Within weeks, he was accepted into a carpentry company on a one-month trial. He learned to be charming and helpful with colleagues and customers, and within weeks was accepted by the manager who increased his salary, but only slightly.

He and Emma moved to a flat and relished the privacy. They even had sex in the shower once as a celebration.

\*\*\*\*\*\*\*\*\*\*\*\*\*\*\*\*\*\*\*\*

She assured him more than once that she was on the right contraception. Then it all went wrong.

'I've got to tell you something, Charlie. Let's go to the pub.' Sitting with their beer and wine drinks she said, 'I'm pregnant.' He was so shocked. It was the last thing he wanted. He tried not to show his anger, his sense that she had let him down.

'Emma. Don't say we'll have to return to Lincoln.'

'No. Of course not. But it'd be a good life for our baby.' He wondered why he was saying this, but it was clear that she would not be doing that.

He packed all his clothes after she'd left for work next day and started the long drive up to Lincolnshire. He told no one at the farm about the pregnancy. The farm was continuing to prosper. His sister had developed a business to do with cows' milk. No need now to milk cows with hands, and she was making cheese. He wasn't sure how.

\*\*\*\*\*\*\*\*\*\*\*\*\*\*\*\*\*\*\*\*

Knowing he had to act quickly he got a job in training Labrador dogs for the blind.

It was many months later that he went to see Emma. He had ignored her earlier messages and they ceased long before the birth. He arrived at what was once their shared flat and she opened the door. The baby was in some sort of carrier, snuggling to her breasts. He became moved by the little creature thinking of its links with Lincolnshire and London. He touched its head and said, 'Boy or girl?'

Emma replied, 'Is it your business?'

'Well, yes, it is. I want to share...'

'No. No. I've got a new partner now.' He knew it was all his fault, and left immediately.

*********************

On the way home, he thought about an old school friend who had joined the Army. Yes. Yes. The more he thought about it as he drove through the last edges of London, it started to seem the right thing for him to do. It would get him away. No rent. No upkeep, and along with all this there was a feeling that he would be respected. Goodbye life on the farm, and apologies for not attending college in London. He'd have to log out. He'd be marching, wearing uniform. The military, the military, and generally he would be respected, sometimes highly respected.

Great idea. I might be driving that way now, but I certainly wasn't going back to life on the farm. I'd done okay with that intelligent Labrador, but it would have to be returned. I'm sure they'd find another trainer. It was getting close to being ready to befriend a blind person.

He was out of town and into green and gold fields. All the harvesting being busily carried out. Such incredible equipment to hand now. No need to build huge haystacks and pay firms to bring thrashing machines to separate the wheat from the hay. Then the soil will have to be ploughed and new things planted. I don't want it. I want routine but not that. The

Army. Yes. That little creature was with Emma now. Move on. Move on.

********************

He drove on switching to thoughts of enlisting and relishing his freedom to choose. Saw himself in uniform and moving to foreign countries, then he started humming to a brass band. His foot was going down on the accelerator. It was a broad, 3 lane road, and he moved to the fast lane, then honked at one vehicle forcing it to move to middle. His spirits were rising, his distress declining. Then he jerked as a large vehicle seemed to be almost stationary in the fast lane. He veered into the middle lane, felt another vehicle hitting him from behind. His car seemed to be somersaulting. He knew no more.

# Story 2: That

'What are we going to do if we don't do that?'

'Lucas. I've made my mind up to do THAT.' She stressed the word as if it was full of potential adding.

'I hear you've been looking more at places in this city.' There was a pause.

'But, Lucas, we've done all that. We've thought about the advantages and disadvantages and surely, we've made our minds up.' She half knew he was a bit undecided.

'Yep. Remember we nearly went for the one up hill near the park. You're not listening.'

'Yes, I am. Yes, yes, we did go twice to see that one.'

There was silence as he focussed on his scrambled egg. She added, 'But it was the cottage we decided to go for.'

She stood up, leaving him at the table as she prepared to get to her work in the library. More talk this evening. He watched her donning her weatherproof jacket. 'Raining?'

'Yep. Bye, love.' She kissed the top of his head, and he heard the door close and key turn. She walked to her car feeling on the grim side. She wanted to be out of this city, all the traffic and bad air. A different life in the country. A new life.

The good life.

*********************

'So, you're moving to Cornwall?'

Her friend at work had a mixture of shock and disapproval in her tone.

'Yep. On the verge. It's near Yeovil, south Somerset area,'

'Wherever that is.'

Liz turned back to her computer screen, finding herself thinking of Lucas and his sudden doubts about THAT move, which she knew was what she wanted.

*********************

When she got home after work that day, she was preparing a beef lasagne with a red wine bottle already on the table. Usually they drank wine only at weekends, starting Friday evening.

He came home looking at her immediately, before taking his leather jacket off. 'I've had a salary increase. Actually, rather a lot. I've decided to go for it along with whatever you want. There's only one tricky thing and that's to do with the cottage but I'm going to continue my work here and get a small flat near the office.'

So, he wanted to treat the cottage as a weekend get-away, but she wanted 100% commitment to this rural abode. They would work on an orchard which was presently overgrown… perhaps chickens and soon have a family and get the children to that primary school which was within walking distance. They both had a car. He could get local work. There was a library in Yeovil, but she might put her time into growing fruit and vegetables and perhaps having a market stall. She could do part time at the library. She poured them both a glass of wine and said, 'Cheers. Well done.' It was good news and his increase in salary would certainly help them financially. Selling this place would be a help too. This present apartment had been rated high. They laughed together, enjoyed the lasagne, and went to bed quite early, taking the wine with them.

Then sex, followed by sleepiness.

She awoke, smiling to herself. Would he gradually be seduced by that rural delight. She'd just had a dream about them having 2 children and they'd both gone to that local riding school she'd noticed about half a mile from the cottage, and in her dream, she was thinking of buying a horse for herself. She smiled now thinking she could rent a meadow close to the cottage. If they moved, he might gradually decide to get work there. She turned in bed beside him, but he'd already gone.

*********************

A few weeks later the shock came. She was pregnant. Missed three periods and told no one, but her pregnancy had been confirmed. She knew it was to do with the lovely three weeks holiday they'd had in Normandy, when they'd enjoyed the beach in Fecamp, and visited that fascinating museum in Bayeux where the Bayeux Tapestries were displayed. All that history in 1066 when William, Duke of Normandy challenged Harold 11 King of England and won the battle. The Saxon army was destroyed and William, Duke of Normandy took the crown. Yes. This pregnancy. Indeed. It was all her fault –

she'd forgotten to pack her contraceptives. They'd agreed. No sex, but it didn't happen. They'd been so happy together on this holiday, and finding French restaurants a delight, and loving all the small towns and villages and enjoying so much time with each other.

'Liz. I'm back. More good news.'

What was all that about? Their moving house?

'I've been promoted. Even bigger increase in salary. We need to buy a mansion here.'

'Heck.'

'Why heck?'

He was now sitting across from her. She thought about how good looking he was, a term her mother often used.

'Lucas, I'm pregnant.'

His blue eyes looked at her as if she was awesome.

'That's got to be good news.'

'Yeah, all to do with my mistakes in Normandy, my careless packing.'

'Don't blame yourself. I was there as well. Our NO SEX was not obeyed.'

She felt flushes of pleasure. 'Yep. Together, together.'

He grinned. 'We'll get there.'

They both stood up and moved towards each other. Then embraced.

It was all clear now. They wouldn't be doing THAT.

# Story 3: Dangling

I'm not sure where I was born but have been told I was in an orphanage when I was adopted by my present parents. I was age 3. They had two sons, age 8 and 11, and by the time I was in secondary school one was in the Army and one at university. Always thought I ought to go after one or the other, but I left school, age 16 and got working for a butcher guy who had a large shed-like place where dead animals were brought, and workers got them all prepared for his various butcher shops.

After a short time there, I learned how to turn dead animals into sellable portions of meat, like legs, chops, ribs, steak, and it involved a lot of hacking and cutting. A foreman-like guy initially instructed me and kept his eye on what I was doing. Then, on that dreadful day I hacked my little finger, or half cut it off. The pain was unbearable, and they got the bleeding me into an ambulance and at the local hospital I was immediately put in a ward and an x-ray was done. It took many days to go through the various processes of getting "pinky", as they called it, back into a reasonable state. I had apparently damaged the bone as well as the flesh, as I thought of it, and had to have anaesthetic while they used plates or wires to get the finger back to its normal state. Eventually I went back to my parents but had regular hospital checks and physiotherapy appointments. There was something about seeing my little finger hanging there, the shock of it, and the thoughts of it haunted me, wouldn't go away. I had an awful dream one night that it was my penis, my willy, that was half cut off and left dangling uselessly, like a leaf in autumn, preparing to drop and disappear back into the earth. So, I had no job for several weeks, although the butcher manager did offer me some return stuff, but no way could I return to that place.

Then a job came. Newsagents, morning deliveries to the elderly or disabled. That worked okay and I made friends with many recipients, and they used to invite me in for tea and biscuits, but then the boss suddenly told me I wasn't covering enough addresses. Job lost.

Then job number three and I got involved with that criminal guy and finished up nine months in prison.

\*\*\*\*\*\*\*\*\*\*\*\*\*\*\*\*\*\*\*\*\*

It's three months now since I was discharged, and I knew I should never have been there. What the f…was he doing, my boss? While I was doing the gardening, car cleaning and dog walking tasks, for these elderly or disabled people, he would have searched out their cash hordes. He frequently called into these homes, while I was working. They paid him and he paid me. He was the thief, and me the job doer, but I was seen in court as aiding and abetting. Shit! It was a nightmare in my prison cell where, as you can imagine, I looked frequently at my little finger which sometimes was my friend as it was doing well, but frequently it averted me to thoughts of a dangling penis.

My job now is Community work for the Council, which is mainly emptying bins which were in abundance along the seafront esplanade. I also had a tool to pick up litter scattered on street pavements urrgh… uneaten chips, cigarette ends, half-finished plastic coffee mugs, those old-fashioned condoms and, of course, dog poo.

Yeah… it was a relief getting home and out of that tiny cell. I was now approaching my 19th birthday and my parents were talking about it, and had arranged for a little family gathering, one brother, as the Army one was abroad, somewhere near the Ukraine border. My adoptive grandparents were all coming and the Uni. brother was bringing his girlfriend.

I've now started attending a gym and do these strenuous exercises 3 times a week. I've met two guys there who were also in the group when this chap welcomed us in and gave us exercise instructions. We all did well. They apparently worked on a building site and talked a lot about more workers being needed. After several months, I started to go with them for a drink in a close-by pub. They often mentioned sex, but I grinned and never said I'd never done it. Not with another person but I knew I wanted it. It was time to move on. To get a woman, get a woman. When I looked in that long mirror in my bedroom, I could see my body was good. Muscles, biceps, as the chap called it, all now was clear to the eye. I knew it was time to move on.

The birthday thing happened. Nobody made a fuss of me, but food and drinks were in abundance. Grandparents never had given me much attention except always buying presents at birthdays and Xmas. My brother's girlfriend talked to me a lot. She was a right good looker. Her face was a bit doll like but she had lovely long slim legs and pert assertive looking tits.

*********************

I was there again with them in the pub, drinking our half pints, feeling fit after an hour of gym exercises. They were both in their tight jeans and leather jackets. My jeans were looser and no leather jacket, just an anorak.

'My turn,' Greg said.

'No, mine,' Frank grinned and nodded towards the woman who was standing in a corner near the door, with some sort of drink on a ledge. We hadn't seen her here before.

'Reckon, she's up for grabs.'

Frank spoke raising his eyebrows then did what he did frequently. Checked his mobile before slipping it into his jeans back pocket. I was curious.

'What you two on about?' I took a good look at the woman. She had a way of standing there as if she didn't mind or respond to the looks.

Greg grinned at Frank. 'Not a good idea, never know what you might catch.'

'Too late, mate.'

The woman had moved off with a tall, well dressed, white haired, man. Frank started talking to me about the building site and my concentration turned towards getting more information on their tasks. Sometime later I noticed the woman was now settling back in the same place and was reaching for her drink on the ledge. Pete looked at me.

'Yeah, my turn, mate, but I'm just off to the loo.' I moved off quickly wondering if my turn could be this woman. I winked at her and she kind of responded by half smiling and moving her eyes towards a little door, which I always thought was private and for pub owners only.

Meanwhile as I thought Greg would be ordering out final half pints.

It was some time before I headed back to the bar and could see the three half pints were already there. By the time I'd been to the loo, I could see the woman was now settling back in the same place.

I had a surging feel of satisfaction. Job done. Job done.

'Sorry, guys. Was my turn but I've spent it. No dosh.'

I couldn't help grinning as I reached for my anorak on a nearby stool.

'What! You been with her?'

I couldn't help grinning. 'See you on Tuesday.' I walked towards exit.

'That's him gone. Do you reckon he did it?'

'Yep, and she's just moved to sit down at a table and is ordering food and wine.'

'Shall we share the beer we bought for him.'

'What with her?'

'Certainly not.'

'Okay. Why not.' He took a sip of half pint number three.

I walked off along the pavement looking down at my little finger. It seemed to be wagging at me, saying, well done.

*Well,* I thought, *little pinky is right.* I gave it a kiss.

# Story 4: Sixties

'I can't believe this is happening...' she was muttering to herself as she picked another egg out of the fridge.

'Mum, are you talking to yourself or is it me wanting two eggs?'

'No, Anne. It's something else. I'll tell you sometime. Nothing to do with your eggs. I'll get them poaching.'

'When's Alice coming?'

'Not until ten today. You going to work in your car?'

'Of course, Mum.'

'So, it's going well.'

Anne didn't reply as she'd started to read a novel and brought it down from her bedroom. She was entranced and couldn't leave a chapter unfinished. 'Here you are, eggs done. I'm going to take the corgis for a run around...have got the Women's Institute meeting here today.'

'Okay.'

Marian looked across at her daughter, as she picked up the corgi's leads.

'Anne. There's something important I want to say. We'll do it this evening.'

'I won't be here, Mum. I've got a date, as we all call it.'

Marian didn't reply. The corgis were snuggling against her legs. This was the second time she'd mentioned this intention. 'Bye Mum. I'll be gone when you get back.'

She let the corgis run free as she walked across their spacious lawn and into the orchard. As she stood at the gate the dogs started to bark with excitement. Intelligent little creatures, they knew the walk was happening. She continued to let them run free as she walked across the field towards the pond and their yapping came again as they galloped towards a group of ducks pecking around at the pond edges. As usual, the ducks confidently moved into the water, swimming rapidly towards the centre area, seeming to know they were safe there. She called the corgis, and they ran back to her, as usual, expecting the nibble delights she would give them. Then with leads on she walked briskly towards an area of ploughed fields, glancing at her watch. Women's Institute meeting this morning. Alice would be there by then, and yesterday had got the lounge room ready, and would bring in the coffee, tea and biscuits at the appropriate time. She tightened her mouth as she thought about the agenda. It was a relatively new group as earlier she had belonged to the local town group, and then decided it would be good to get a group started in this very rural area. There'd been a lot of questions about what it would be about, and she'd stressed that being a member means you want to make a difference in this community. It would be sectarian and non-political. We can do art, craft, cookery etc. We could arrange quizzes and invite speakers.

She began to hurry home thinking Charles would be back tomorrow afternoon. He was away for a two-day session at a Farmers Union conference. There was a dispute to do with the

CPRE wanting to re-establish footpaths which had been ignored by some, and all the Public Footpath signs taken down by many local landowners.

After the WI meeting, which went well, Marian got a phone call from Anne saying she'd be home and had cancelled her date.

'Can't say anymore, Mum…work is busy.'

Marian felt relieved. Some things had to be said. She thought about Susan who'd been at a previous WI meeting, after which they had relaxed and drank a second cup of coffee together. Susan had described the coming up wedding of her son. Sounded amazing. It was going to be at the city cathedral and then back to the local village Hall. She'd hired caterers and was insisting her son had a new tailor-made suit.

'Sounds great.'

'Yes. It's what I've always wanted.'

'I'd like that too.' Marian thought it most likely this wouldn't happen.

Evening came and Anne appeared with a wide smile on her face.

'Hi, Mum. I've got to tell you.'

'She dangled her left hand under the light.'

'We're engaged.'

'What!'

'Yes. Simon's a great guy. Don't think you've ever met him.'

'Hmm…I know, Anne. You've mentioned him before. He's the son of the village blacksmith, Fred Brooks. Apparently, they've got 7 children.'

'Yeah. He always talks about being one of seven.'

Marian was trying to control her disapproval. This was ridiculous, but what could she do. Anne was nearly 20 now. Ridiculous yes, but she had another really important issue to discuss with Anne, but clearly now was not the time. 'Anne, I think you're too young to make decisions like this...you're still a teenager.' *Only on the verge of being 20* Marian thought.

'I am not. I am not.'

She was shaking her head and added.

'We're going to have a registry office wedding and then just leave and go on a holiday together.'

'I think you're too young to make decisions like this.'

'I'm not.' She was nodding.

'But, Anne...'

'No buts, Mum. Look, we're in the sixties. So many things are changing. My friends laugh about it...I guess I knew you'd...' Marian paused.

'Mum. I'll bring Simon round to meet you and Dad.'

'Anne. You can't do this. Your father won't agree.'

'I knew you'd say this but you've got to move on. Like I said, things are changing. Makes me laugh when I think about how class was such a serious thing. Arranged marriages. God! Not for me those days and just think, now we have contraception and all that...Anyway, I'll leave you to take it in...might take time. Simon and I would rent in the city.'

When Anne left, Marian poured herself a double brandy. Then reprimanded herself, took one small sip and emptied the remains in the geranium plant pot.

********************

110

The next day when Charles returned, he was overwhelmed with indignation about the CPRE demands.

'What's the world coming to? Our land, our business not theirs. Sounds splendid Council for the Preservation of Rural England. What a lot of bollocks!' Marian felt 100% behind him. Why should any member of the public be able to walk across their land? Their Manor House acres.

'They say if we don't come to some agreement, they will take the case to court.'

'What!'

'I know. It doesn't make sense.'

'Yes. I do remember you moving one of those Public Footpath signs just after your father died.'

'Ah…several, I reckon.'

'That was years ago.'

'Things were different then. Not many had cars.'

'True. True.'

'No more of all that.' He looked at her, his eyes focussing on hers. 'Marian,

Marian, more importantly, how have you been?'

'Much the same, Charles. Think we're still on the way.'

'Good. I must go now. They're all turning up for the beet singling.' He kissed the top of her head and bustled out.

\*\*\*\*\*\*\*\*\*\*\*\*\*\*\*\*\*\*\*\*

At the next WI meeting in the vicarage, 3 new women turned up, although one didn't stay, quietly slipping out after half an hour. The woman she had come in with said, 'Apologies. I'll say more later.' To Marian's surprise the third one was Ada Brooks, and she struggled to calm herself.

Ada spoke with a very local accent saying, 'I be useful…cooking and stuff.'

'Anything else you want from the group?' Marian heard herself saying,

'Sure, there'll be other things. B'in in this village – was born here.'

'Were you really?' Gladys said.

'Yeah…and 'ave 7 children born ere'

Marian looked at two of the regular members and they were responding to Ada in a very friendly welcoming way, asking about her children, the schools they'd attended and their lives now. Looking at her watch Marian decided it was time for a coffee break, and it was the responsibility of Florence, chairperson today, to call this. For some reason, she began to think about the group in the local town. It wasn't like that here, but it would take time. She looked across at Ada, thinking of Anne and what was his name. Stephen. No. It was Simon. Did Ada know about all this? Probably not. Rubbish. Yes, she did.

No, she didn't.

Marian shuffled uneasily, looking again at her watch. Then, to her surprise, the other new woman said she needed to tell us something. The group listened. 'You all saw the woman who came in with me.' They nodded. 'Well, we're together.'

'You renting a place?' Someone asked, trying to be friendly.

'No. It's her cottage.'

Marian said, 'Well, that's okay. Perhaps she'll come to our next meeting.'

'The truth is, we're in love.'

Everything went quiet, no one responded, and they all started looking at their watches.

'Coffee and tea time,' Florence said.

Marian went home thinking about these two, well what were they? Queers? No, they were lesbians. Was it legal now to be sexually united, or did they just cuddle each other a lot and kiss. She thought of Oscar Wilde and what happened to him. Imprisoned, but that was long ago. She heard Anne's voice, It's the sixties Mum, everything's changing. Why shouldn't same sex couples fall for each other.

\*\*\*\*\*\*\*\*\*\*\*\*\*\*\*\*\*\*\*\*\*

A few days later when Charles was meeting some of his Farmers' Union friends in the pub, Anne came in from work and Marian touched her shoulder as she was about to go up to her room.

'Anne. There's something I have to tell you.'

'Okay, Mum. Make me a mug of tea.'

'Sit down. I'll bring it.'

As they both sat holding their mugs, Marian started.

'You'll be surprised about this. I'm pregnant.'

'What!' Anne spilt some tea on the sofa and took time swabbing it with a tissue.

'You're pregnant, Mum. Are you sure?'

'It's looking very likely. I've missed three periods.'

'And you're…err how old Mum? I remember your fortieth birthday but that was years and years and years ago.'

'I'm 48'

Anne slurped half of the mug.

'So, Anne, you might have a brother or sister, at last.'

'What does Dad say?'

'He's pleased.'

'Well, if you're both pleased…'

'We are. We are.'

'What can I say?'

There was a long pause, until Anne said,

'If it's good news for you and Dad, it's good news for me.'

Marian finished her coffee. It seemed Anne didn't want to say anymore. 'I've got things to do upstairs Mum. I'll be down later. I'm eating our tonight with Simon.' She grinned, 'My-you-know-who.'

Marian continued to sit, rubbing her tummy. She and Charles had gone to a lot of trouble to get, what they hoped they were getting. His sperm, her fertilised egg, all in the laboratory, and inserted now into her uterus, and when she went for her last check, they confirmed it was all going ahead well.

As months went by her pregnancy continued and Charles frequently hugged her, which he hadn't done for years. When her tummy made it all blatantly obvious, she told the WI group she was expecting a child, but said nothing about the conception.

When the birth of the boy came, Charles was beside her in her hospital bed. He quickly held the new baby in his arms. 'Marian. You're wonderful. I'm proud of you.'

The next day he visited and lifted the baby from his cot, holding him in a loving kind of way, touching his tiny hands and kissing him gently on his forehead. 'What's his name going to be?' He sat down beside his wife's bed, then handed their new son to her. They looked at each other grinning with optimism. '…and, Marian, you might think I'm acting too soon but along with a few other farmers, we've agreed to go along with the CPRE.'

Marian frowned, as he took their son back to the cot, thinking perhaps she was being too old fashioned.

'Well, if you're sure.'

He didn't answer as Anne came into the ward.

'Mum. What great news. I can't believe it.'

'You have a brother, Anne.'

'Wow!'

She walked round to the cot and peered down at the baby.

\*\*\*\*\*\*\*\*\*\*\*\*\*\*\*\*\*\*\*\*

Yes. *Things really were changing,* she thought, as she was settling into their mansion house with their son, Lucas. It was all unbelievable, making her smile. Charles was out there this morning with a person working for the CPRE, putting up the PUBLIC FOOTPATH signs. The WI had agreed to have those two lesbians as members, and Anne had been so wrapped in her baby brother, and only yesterday said,

'Me and Simon are still on but not getting married, although we'll be living together in the city and I've got and he's got work there.'

Marian picked up her new baby boy and prepared to breast feed, something that was going well.

*It was the sixties,* she thought, *and everything was turning out rosy.*